ARTHUR

Legends of the King

Kevin's
both

Mike

ARTHUR

Legends of the King

MICHAEL KERR SCOTT

First published in 2013 in China by Foreign Language and Teaching Press as Ten Stories of King Arthur

This edition published in 2017 by Albert Bridge Books

For Eirlys and all she loved

CONTENTS

Preface: The Once and Future King viii

One: Idris and Arthur 1
Two: Eagles and Bears 8
Three: The Riddle of the Lake 15
Four: Rhita Gawr..37
Five: Sir Gawain and the Green Knight............50
Six: Merlin's Tree 84
Seven: Lancelot and Gawain 90
Eight: Ogof Y Meirw...99
Nine: The Release of Merlin 115
Ten: Crossing the Ravine 147

Some Welsh Words..166
References 169

Preface

The Once and Future King

The great stories of the world transcend both time and place. They are passed on from generation to generation, each framing them by and with its own will, conditions, ideology and technology. On 31st July 1485 William Caxton published Sir Thomas Malory's assemblage of chivalric Arthurian romances, *Le Morte D'Arthur,* many of which had come or returned to England from a French tradition. What Malory did, as Eugène Vinaver pointed out in his edition of Malory's *Works* in 1971, was to create a "singleness" for the stories, a narrative which "underlies the normal structure of a modern work of fiction."

Centuries before Malory, however, the Arthurian legend was being passed on orally and in script in wider and differing cultural contexts than those represented in his work. Celtic tales from Wales, for example, presented a more ambiguous Arthur than the later chivalric one: a warrior of the mountains and valleys, linked with animals and birds, "Arthur…bear of the host, joy of sight,/the eagle has seen you before." But he is a leader who is possessed also with supernatural attributes. This is a man about whom sagas should be written, rich in his uncertain passage between life and death. The King's resting place may be lost or it may be all around us in a sentiment summed up in an enigmatic line from an Old Welsh text, "Anoeth bid bet y Arthur," which possibly translates as, "The world's wonder a grave for Arthur."

The new technology of Caxton's press, however, fixed Malory's version as the dominant tradition of Arthurian expression. It prompted over centuries new creativity with, for example, Edmund Spenser's allegorical *Faerie Queene* at the end of the sixteenth century or the Victorian poems by Alfred Lord Tennyson and Matthew Arnold. Historically, Kings of England, particularly of the Tudor dynasty, even considered and attempted to fashion themselves as being of the Arthurian chivalric lineage.

The other myths, as valid as those of the Malory tradition, were not lost as they lay dormant. The English fourteenth-century alliterative poem, *Sir Gawain and the Green Knight* and the older, rich Welsh narratives did not die. To this day the names of mountains, hills and valleys in Wales and elsewhere retain reference to the legend and the expression of the Celtic myths beneath.

The stories in this volume can be read as tales on their own but they also come together providing a narrative continuity or "singleness." They draw on stories and characters from the various traditions in a manner that contemporary artists or composers freely feed from paintings or music scores from the past, amalgamating aspects of one with another to produce works which are new and fresh and possessing an integrity of their own. Old tales here are freely retold and embellished and are included with newly created ones by the author within a framing context of the mythical Welsh god, Idris. He is given five daughters, one of whom, Morgen, has rebelled against him. She, reminiscent perhaps of a number of literary forebears as, for example, Morgan le Fay and Vivien, is nevertheless a new character. She is a traditional but wayward elemental force: the malignant, revengeful daughter of the god, manifested in the cruelty of wind and tempest.

In the early seventeenth century the satirist, John Marston, exposing courtly hypocrisy wrote, "…there's a Lady Guinevere bears up that Sir Lancelot. Dreams, dreams, visions, fantasies, chimeras, imaginations, tricks, conceits!" The dreams, visions and conceits of the Arthurian myth reveal issues that each generation has to put into context. The most simple things are sometimes the most profound. Leadership, care and responsibility battling with their antitheses are at the heart of the legend whenever and however it is expressed. Then there are the matters also of betrayal, conscience and memory.

The Welsh poet and dramatist, Saunders Lewis, living in the twentieth century characterised by the horrors of two world wars and the knowledge of the atrocity of which humanity is capable, wrote, "Remember? I remember too much. There is no pain/Like the pain of failing to forget in the nightmare of being."

In the new stories presented here, Merlin's imprisonment in the pain of what was and what is, has to be excised. He has to be released from his tree, from the anguish of memory. The world can learn from but cannot live with the destructive stasis found in the anguish of its mistakes. It has to be freed, to move on from generation to generation, soaring high above the mountain tops accepting its flight, its progress as the precious force it is.

King Arthur weaves his magic but there is the point. It is not Arthur but the stories old and new of King Arthur which are "the once and future King," the endurance recreation and development of the myth itself, in whatever form or tradition or combination from age to age, country to country, place to place, wherever the trials and attributes depicted and woven apply.

Old life, new life, a little bird healed of its affliction flies from the cave of living into the world and we use the memory of what once was to help protect the good in what is. In the final two stories, Corwen's bell rings out for both sides of the ravine.

Michael Kerr Scott,
Oxford.
May 2017.

ONE

IDRIS AND ARTHUR

So it was that all the Chieftains of the land having failed to withdraw the sword from the stone, gathered with Merlin, the Counsellor of the realm, in the great hall. They were considering what was to be done since the Head Chieftain or King could not be proclaimed without the royal weapon being freed from the rock. It was then that Arthur, the son of Dragonhead, entered the hall with the sword in his hand.

"Is this what you need to proclaim the King?" he asked.

Everyone stared in amazement. Merlin seeing the sword in the young boy's hand immediately signalled all to fall to their knees and swear loyalty to Arthur for this time now and for all time their King.

"Arthur, our King," they proclaimed with one voice, though a few silently seethed with anger, believing that the boy and Merlin had tricked them in some way. Merlin knew their thoughts and cried out, "Who saw Arthur pull the sword cleanly from its stone sheath fast locked in the great rock?"

Three knights known for their honesty and integrity who had entered the hall with the boy, proclaimed that they and the people standing around the stone had witnessed it all. Merlin ordered that the whole gathering should return to the rock and when they arrived the people themselves called out that Arthur was their King for now and evermore, just as the Chieftains had done. Dissent in individual hearts was dispelled but not the envy and jealousy. It was such envy which was shared by the followers of Morgen, the errant daughter of Idris, the progenitor of all that is, was and is to come.

In the beginning Idris had risen from the earth in a torrent of fire bringing with him the great mountain Cadair Idris. He fought the god of the north lands whose wife he married bearing him five daughters: Seren, Morwen, Tanwen, Corwen and Morgen, the last of whom rebelled against him.

Following the adventure with the sword in the stone, Merlin met again with the boy at a cairn or burial place which overlooks the sea across to Ireland. It was cold and dreary but Arthur had spent the night there, not worried about the curse allegedly put upon anyone who should sleep in such a fearful place. "Are you not frightened," Merlin asked, "to have slept on the stones that some believe are a memorial to our ancestors?" "Why should I be," the boy replied, "if they were of our blood, no harm will come to me." He knew well the curse of madness that might ensue from the cairn on which he'd slept but also that it could be a curse of love, and that one day such love might destroy him. He anticipated the risks that were to come but understood that first he would have to endure a ritual to assume his power fully. He asked Merlin from where his new Kingly authority originated. Merlin recognised the question as a sign of wisdom and asked the boy whether he had seen any visions whilst he slept. Arthur replied that he had dreamt of a great mountain that he had to climb.

"Then that," Merlin replied, "is the answer to your question. The mountain called Cadair Idris, is the throne of

Idris and that is where we must go." Merlin, with a forced smile, tried to conceal his anxiety about the ordeal of the ritual which the boy was to face but he couldn't deceive Arthur. "It's only a mountain, Merlin, only a mountain," the young King laughed as he strode down the path towards the river and then onwards in the direction of Cadair Idris. They arrived just after midday with Merlin suggesting that they might wait and rest so as to ascend to the summit the next day but Arthur was determined that the climb should begin immediately so that they could see the sunset from the highest peak. The day was calm, the sky flecked by wisps of clouds allowing the golden light through onto the valley of the River Mawddach. Arthur eagerly scrambled up the terrain with Merlin lagging behind. The old Counsellor already admired and loved the boy but was fearful for him as he has continued to be, in his care of him, throughout time. Arthur was a natural leader. Indeed he was already leading Merlin on a climb which would result in the confirmation of his power by the mighty Idris. But he had an innocence about him, a naivety in the faith of the inherent goodness of all people. This concerned Merlin, as out of breath he watched the boy scampering along, never looking down but always upwards until he reached a cliff face that barred the route to the top. It was there that the young King waited for the Counsellor who produced ropes and metal stakes which he hammered into the rocks, to help them make their ascent.

So it was that Arthur already acclaimed by the people as King was taken by Merlin to the highest point on Cadair Idris from where he looked into the setting sun. The light almost blinded him but in the centre of the reddening sphere he saw the figure of Idris along with four of his daughters: Morwen of the Sea, Seren of the Stars, Tanwen of the Fire and Corwen of the White Rock. There the great god encircled by his progeny stared back at Arthur and commissioned him to lead his people in defence of their lands now invaded by the rough tribes from the North. The god, Idris, solemnly raising his arms and coming out of the sun, threw down lightning shafts on Arthur which in the intensity of their heat threw the boy to the ground, instilling in him the six attributes of his kingship: wisdom, strength, courage, counsel, endurance and justice. He granted Arthur two gifts. First the power of the gods, with which when required the King might transform himself and his warriors into whatever creatures he desired, whether lions or bears, eagles or dolphins, mice or spiders. Second when the time might come Idris granted the boy a blessing to defy death through a sleep, guarded by Corwen his daughter, from which Arthur could be awakened as the world might require or Idris might dictate.

Arthur having fallen to his knees, the pain of the heat still being endured, humbly accepted the god's solemn covenant as witnessed by Merlin. But Arthur knew that all was not as it should be. Why could he only see four of Idris' daughters not five? So with courage and determination, the young King spoke out his concern. Where was the fifth of the daughters?

"You should be five not four," he bravely called out to the women once again circling their father who had returned into the sun. "Five not four," he repeated, "and so where is the fifth?"

Merlin held Arthur's arm begging him to say no more since such things were not to be asked or contemplated but the boy rejected the Counsellor's pleading insisting that if he was to lead as King, then all had to be revealed whatever the cost. Idris looked down in sadness and anguish as rolling his head from side to side the sun itself began to rock this way and that.

"Quick, quick," Merlin called, "let me tie you to a rock before Morgen of the Winds comes. You called for her and you must be prepared to withstand her consuming evil."

The old Counsellor took the boy, whose eyes were still fixed on those of the god, and fastened him with ropes to a rock as tight as he could. The winds began to blow across that desolate height, from which Merlin retreated scaling down the mountain as fast as he could, leaving the secured boy to the mercy of the gods.

Arthur could feel a storm gathering about him and through the growing darkness clouds circled around and moved inwards towards him. He looked up to the sinking sun, straining to see the figures in the dying light as the blackness of the clouds on the horizon gathered pace towards the land.

"Don't leave me," he wanted to cry out but remained silent as Idris and the four daughters faded from sight in the gathering gloom and an uncomfortable, hostile stillness descended. Arthur began to test the strength of the bonds that Merlin had tied, struggling against them but they held him fast. "Oh," he thought, "why was I so foolish as to tempt Idris so with my question?" Behind his rock he heard a movement, and then was sickened by a stench that filled the air, a stomach turning smell of rotting flesh.

"Who's there?" he called as the winds began to blow again within which he could hear a shrill whistling accompanying the sound of moving feet in the greyness of the terrain. There were no sunrays now to help, only the twilight over the vulnerable earth. Frightened, he listened as the whistling turned to a screeching and as the sound of the footsteps intensified. On and on the unseen feet danced as if summoning the winds to blow harder and harder until with the same momentum the rains arrived lashing Arthur's face and body. Within minutes the winds escalated to the force of a gale which throughout the night tore at his clothes, shredding them and leaving his naked body exposed to the biting, razor sharp rain. It whipped him this way and that across his face, his arms, his chest and his legs. As the winds changed direction, the rains followed so that no part of his body escaped the lashing. Even the cords securing him severed throwing him to the ground where the biting rains inflicted further pain on his back increasing his torment. The noise was deafening as the shriek of the voice in the air became one with the elements. It was as he cried for mercy that he heard a cruel laughter which struck him to the very soul but undaunted he cried out again calling on Idris and instantly the clouds dispersed, the laughter ceased and the sun rose in the East.

Wretched and bleeding, he looked up to where Idris and the four daughters were peering to the West and then lifting himself up onto all fours like an animal, Arthur followed their gaze in the direction of the retreating winds and saw a hideous woman, like a rotten corpse, dancing and revelling in her moment of sadistic cruelty. She was bent double, with a whiskered chin and her revengeful eyes glared back at him from her leprous face. Arthur understood the enormity of an evil that had reduced him to crawling on the ground. Struggling to lift himself, the look of perverted triumph on her face so angered him that it gave him a new strength and holding onto the rock, the young King raised himself. Standing tall he defied the corpse like witch, ignoring the pain of his wounds and fuelled by the determination of his will, King Arthur cried out, "I know you, foul witch of the Winds, Morgen betrayer of all the good in Idris. I know you for what you are and will defy you till the end of time, as bare, naked and lacerated as I am."

At that Idris bathed the boy in golden light, healing his wounds and the four daughters appeared on the mountain before him, tending to him and clothing him in leathers and furs whilst Morgen withdrew into the winds and vanished into nothingness.

It was then that Arthur staggering in his exhaustion was helped by the four sisters to a nearby level rock where he lay down to rest. Here he slept dreaming of Morwen, Seren, Tanwen and Corwen and when he awoke on the summit of that mighty mountain, they had all gone but Merlin had returned to tend to him.

"So it is," Merlin said, "that your commission has been given, your rite of kingship endured and your work has begun."

"And you?" Arthur asked.

"Me?" Merlin replied. "Why, in the world's way you will lose me just as you will lose all the others except Idris and his four daughters."

They looked to the sun but neither Idris nor his daughters appeared. They had been seen, Arthur had experienced the reality of a vision and now he was left alone with the remembrance. As the two men descended the mountain, they passed a tree the top of which was covered with mistletoe, grown black and knotted over the years. Merlin shuddered and rushed on.

"What is it?" the King enquired.

"My future," the old Counsellor replied.

They reached the foot of the mountain and continued onwards into the stories that follow and many more.

Two

Eagles and Bears

Was it true that Arthur could transform himself into a beast, a bear or a bird? Read on and decide for yourself through the story of Tagit and the coming of eagles and bears.

Young Tagit was known to everyone as Tag. His mother's name was Non and his father was called Tagit the Red because of his red hair and beard. They were good, honest people who lived near Pengwern which today is called Shrewsbury. They were Old Britons who had been forced West by Anglo Saxon invaders but a truce had been secured between the invaders and King Arthur which meant that they felt safe enough even in their remote land. In case of attack, however, the King had promised to come to their aid. They hunted the land and grew their own food but were always watchful. Tag's sister, whose name was Manon, was young and beautiful and he loved her greatly. She was older than him and could ride a horse better than a grown man. She would ride seated or flat against the horse's back or she could ride on its side, so that she could go undiscovered. The family lived in an encampment of wooden houses, little more than huts, each of which had beams across the inside of the roof on which were placed straw but in every home there were some false cross beams. These were where the children would be swiftly hidden in case of a sudden attack from the Saxons. Tagit the Red was a Chieftain of the settlement as he had worked with King Arthur to make the truce with the invaders. Tag passed his childhood listening to his mother's songs and his father's tales of the King. He played with his older sister and was content but occasionally his father would pretend that they were being attacked and then he would be lifted into the false rafters where he'd have to lie still until told to come down. In the secret rafters there was food, a knife and drink. During one of these practices Tag opened slightly a crack in the wood so that he could see the family below. His mother knew what he had done but she did not tell his father who thinking it dangerous, would have repaired the gap but his mother would glance up at him and smile and wink continuing with her daily work. When the practice was over, Tag would swing down onto his father's shoulders and outside they'd go and fight with boys similarly seated on their fathers' shoulders, each taking the name of one of King Arthur's great warriors, Tristram, Gawain, Owain, Kay or Pelleas.

Manon would practise riding her horse and in case of attack she was to ride on its side undetected towards the forest. From there she'd mount its back and gallop to King Arthur's camp to ask for aid. The greatest fear was fire since they all believed that the children would be safe unless the village was set ablaze. The King would need to arrive before any fire took hold. So they lived and so they prepared for a day which neither boy nor father thought would come. "A truce is a truce," Tagit the Red would say, "you give your word in an oath and you keep to that oath or words mean nothing."

Tag believed that the rehearsals were just a game but was mistaken. Without warning the Saxons attacked the village advancing across the plain with great speed and ferocity. There was no time for the children to get to the forest so Tag was lifted into the rafters and there remained silent as he'd been trained. Before his father could leave the hut, the entrance was kicked in. He drew his sword but it was knocked from out of his hand. Non was grabbed by two men and forced to her knees, Tag seeing it all through the crack he'd opened. His mother looked up at him to warn him to remain hidden whilst the Saxons pulling back her head forced her to watch as they killed her husband leaving his body by the table, his unsheathed sword at his side. Non didn't utter a word nor did she give her enemies the satisfaction of her crying or screaming. She merely looked with love at the body of her husband on the ground.

Manon, meanwhile, as had been planned, crept out of the house on the far side and mounting her horse, rode on its side. The horse trotted towards the woodland. The men in the hut heard it and ran outside, leaving two of their number behind with Non. The horse galloped away and the men had no interest in following it. They had something else on their mind and did not want to leave the hut for long. When they returned, they went to enjoy the mother who offered no resistance but rather began to play with them. She teased them knowing precious time moved on and she called for music. One of the men produced a pipe and started to play for her to dance upon the table, enchanting them with her beauty as she moved more and more wildly. On hearing the music coming from the hut, men from other huts grew impatient with the women they were abusing and came to see if there was a greater sport. Some of the women they tied up, some were killed and others escaped into the woods. It soon seemed as if all the barbarian camp was crammed in to see Non's wild dance. And so she continued until the Saxon Chieftain became suspicious. He stood up, yelling and shouting around the table then jumped onto it, and so the music stopped. He tore the clothes from Non's body and to the encouraging yells of his companions violently raped her. When he had finished abusing her, he picked her up in the air and threw her to his men as a hunter throws offal to his dogs. The men then followed his cruel example but she made no cry and said nothing. She offered no words and no resistance but even as they grabbed her she tried to play with them in order to gain more time for Arthur to arrive. Her bones were broken in the violence, her body bled and her flesh was torn. When the Chieftain pulled off his men, his hounds, she was almost unrecognisable but she was alive. She had been shamed beyond belief and the boy Tag had witnessed it all. Throughout her ordeal she looked occasionally at him and transferred her thoughts to him. The longer she could endure, the safer all the children of the camp would be. She was sacrificing herself for the future of them all and so Tag held back his tears and his anger and remained where he was.

The Chieftain made a space between the men and came up to Tag's mother who was lying on the floor close to his father's body. There was a silence in the hut and in the village as the Chieftain raised his sword to kill her but stopped at the sound of birds flying overhead.

"Look, look," one of the men shouted, "there are eagles flying into the woods."

The Chieftain lowered his sword and anxiously looked at his men as they heard the mighty roar of a huge bear coming out of the forest leading angry bears of every description to form a ring around the camp. At the Chieftain's hesitation, Non looked to Tag and in her shame and love, she signalled for him to close his eyes. She rolled onto her husband's unsheathed sword which she bravely pushed into her heart. The Chieftain saw what she had done and kicked her body with his boot. He and his men all left the hut their swords held high and were immediately attacked by the bears. Tag pulled at the straw in the roof and saw each of the Saxons butchered, their swords ineffective against the bears. The largest of the bears crushed the invaders one by one in its paws until at last, of the whole tribe, only the Chieftain was left. He was the one who had killed Tag's father and violently abused his mother. Tag forced his head through the straw of his hideaway and called to the bear, "Kill this man, kill this man for he killed my father and attacked my mother. Kill him, I saw it all, kill him."

The bear growled and turned to the Saxon Chieftain. As Tag watched, the bear turned into a warrior with golden hair. It was their King, it was Arthur and all the bears protecting the village resumed their normal shape as King Arthur's Knights. Tag recognised some of them from the descriptions his father had given in telling the stories of his adventures and so he could identify Pelleas, Tristram, Owain and Gawain amongst the others. The King looked at the Chieftain and said with a sad authority in his voice, "I will not as a bear crush you but rather fight with you, man to man. In that way your evil will be yours alone as the evil of all that has happened in this place."

With that, Arthur drew his sword and the two men fought. Sparks flew as their swords clashed but the fight did not last long. The Chieftain was no match for Arthur since Tag's King was far too strong for this beast and so the boy watched the Saxon Chieftain die at the sword of King Arthur and forcing his head and arms fully through the straw, he cheered when it was all over.

Arthur immediately ran to the hut and swung the boy onto his shoulders. A young Knight was with the King whom Tag had recognised as Gawain. This Knight withdrew the sword from Non's body and then covered both the bodies with his own cloak before lifting Tag from the King's shoulders. They all knelt in respect before the covered bodies of his parents. The King holding the boy's hand all the time said, "I knew your parents well and I counted them as my friends. I witnessed their wedding and you as their son should be proud of them. Your sister rode well and we have rescued some of your family and friends but far too many have died. Your name is Tagit, isn't it?"

"Yes, Sir," the boy answered, "but as I do not have my father's red hair, I am called young Tagit or just Tag."

King Arthur looked at him and said, "You are a wise young man with a mind that has been made old before its time. From now on you will be looked after and have me as your protector and if he is willing, you will serve Gawain who will be as a father to you. He will teach you to defend yourself with arms and though one day you will die, you will live and be with me for ages to come."

"And what of my sister?" Tag asked.

"She was brave," the King replied, "and rode well. She will live with you under the protection of the Queen."

The King turned to Gawain, "Look after the boy and introduce him to Merlin. This child when I have gone will be a great prince, though in his old age he will see tragedy even greater than this tragedy today. Treat him well for his name will be known for ever."

With that Gawain took Tag away from the hut and looked after him until the time came when Tag would help him in his need. But that is the subject of another story. As a golden eagle Arthur came to the villagers' aid, as a bear he fought the barbarian hoard and as a King he defeated their barbaric Chieftain. Not a single child was lost in the attack since Arthur arrived, as Tag's father had planned, before the Saxons could set fire to the village. So it is in the legends of old, Arthur is able to transform himself and his companions into birds or bears or beasts of any kind should the need arise, just as Idris had promised.

THREE

THE RIDDLE OF THE LAKE

Do we betray ourselves or do we betray each other? It was a favourite question of Arthur especially following his encounter with the Chieftain of the lake in the Wandering Wood.

Arthur had decided to leave the Southern camp. Put aside the romantic legends of castles and tournaments and ladies with flowing robes and a tantalising "Do not touch me, I am beauty personified" look. This was a bloody time, a superstitious time, a time of cruelty and transformation. King Arthur's fortresses were built of wood. His camp in the South of the country was firmly and strongly erected on the hillside, protected at the rear by sheer cliff and overlooking the forest plains in front of it. One day the King announced that he wished to visit his fort in the North not far from the great mountain, Cadair Idris. No one was to go with him, just the King alone. He was sometimes like that, too much so. Merlin, had learned to accept him as he was and though advising against, would not dissuade him. Arthur was his own man and the old Counsellor could look after things whilst he was away. So the decision being made, the King rode out of the Southern camp across the plain to the forest lands beyond. These he could and indeed was advised by

Merlin to circumnavigate but he chose not to do so, arrogantly determining to ride through them.

It was a mistake since this was the Wandering Wood, a forest full of paths, all of which led to one same place, a foul smelling, stagnant lake where, like others in the past, Arthur kept ending up whichever way he took. He would then turn and follow a different path, only to arrive back where he had departed from and so try again, with the same result. He attempted to mark the trees so as to avoid passing them more than once, but it proved of little use. He'd find that he'd ride past them time and time again but could do nothing to stop himself or his horse from doing so, much at first to his irritation and then to his anxiety. Even this, however, gave way to acceptance so that even though the smell of the water was nauseating, he decided that he would have to dismount at the lakeside and rest. He stopped at some rocks near a pebbled and brushwood beach which formed the shore of the lake. He fought with his own stomach as it lurched at the smell of the water but nevertheless, he strode over the rocks and down towards the shore. It was then that he heard a huge belching sound from the far side of the water. From the beach, exactly opposite to where Arthur stood, came a great shudder as a man dressed as a Chieftain with a pebbled face, rose out of the ground. Arthur had tethered his horse to a tree or else he would have lost him at the terrifying sight of this horrific looking Giant. No wonder the horse neighed with terror, its eyes firing up with fear, since once out of the ground, this Chieftain must have been ten foot tall.

Arthur, as Merlin would narrate, didn't flinch but bent down and picked up two stones lying in some brushwood by his feet and started to play with them. He threw them into the water, bent down and picked up two more which he skimmed across the water, making one of them bounce ten times. He bent down and chose two more which he used as juggling balls, crouching down as they went into the air to pick up a third and a fourth and a fifth and a sixth, a seventh and an eighth. All this time the Chieftain of the lake, from across the water, observed but said nothing though inwardly he was raging that his presence was being ignored. Eventually he could take no more but still did not let his anger show. He merely called across the water,

"Arthur, what games are you playing?"

Arthur pretended surprise and dropped some of the stones.

"Now look what you've made me do. I was at fifteen. Had I reached eighteen, you'd have disappeared back into the earth."

"Why do you say that?" the Chieftain enquired.

"Because no one can juggle eighteen stones. No one at all, not even you."

"Don't play with me," the Chieftain mocked. "I'm not the one in trouble, you are."

"Why should I be in trouble?"

"For a number of reasons."

"Like?"

"You are petulant for a mighty warrior. Perhaps you have lost the fire in your soul and have returned to the adolescent heat of your youth!"

Arthur, for all his bravado, knew that the Chieftain was right since the King had no ideas except to be petulant and merely to throw stones in the lake or up into the air to catch them again. But he asked once more,

"Like?"

The Chieftain laughed mimicking Arthur as he made the reality clear,

"Like you are lost in the Wandering Wood of paths and no paths. Like you are being overpowered by the stench of the water in front of you. Like your feet have sunk into the clay around you and you cannot move a step."

At this, Arthur looked down at his legs and found that it was not quite as the Chieftain had said. Arthur hadn't sunk into the clay but rather it was as if the earth had started to grow around him, over his feet and up to his shins. Arthur couldn't move his legs at all and therefore he conceded defeat.

"You win," he said. "I am lost. I am overpowered. I am trapped. So there we are. You'd better kill me or torture me or do whatever you want with me because I cannot fight you. Clearly you are a coward and a traitor. A coward because you've trapped someone who people will say in time was a man of honour and renown, without giving him a chance to fight. A traitor because whoever you are, you are a subject to the authority of this land and that authority is solely with me since I am the King of these parts."

"Your tongue is as good as your sword," the Chieftain taunted. "I will give you a test. Release yourself from the ground about you and I will direct you out of the forest but in being released you must promise to return to me with an answer that will one day cleanse this lake of mine, making its water as pure as spring flowers."

"Tell me what I have to answer."

"What is it," the Chieftain asked, "that a woman wants above all else in the world? Search and tell me. You have seven days."

With that the ugly Giant, Chieftain of the lake, returned into the ground leaving Arthur throwing more stones into the air, while the ground beneath him continued to grow slowly around his legs.

Arthur considered the situation and realised he had two things to do. The first was to work out how to free himself from the ground that was growing around his feet and legs and the second was to answer a question as old as the oldest stories of the world. He decided to take it step by step. If he bent down to try to release himself with his hands the probability was that the moving, living earth would entrap his hands and arms and leave him in a helpless situation without any regard to his dignity or authority. He would be reduced to nothing more than a four legged animal like the one he once became on Cadair Idris through the mischief of that hideous witch, Morgen. He wasn't going to have that. So what could he do? He thought about what the Chieftain had said to him. The Giant had talked about "Like this and like that," and in doing so he was only repeating Arthur's own words but what was it the Chieftain had said prior to that? That Arthur had lost his fire, and that he'd returned to adolescent heat. King Arthur realised that this gross creature didn't want him imprisoned as a dog or a cat but that he actually wanted him to escape. There were fallen branches, twigs and brushwood on the living earth and he was holding stones in his hand. He had fire and heat just as he had been taunted.

With that Arthur crouched down at the knees and gathered as much old bracken and brushwood as he could around him. Then using the stone as a flint he hit the other stone over and over so that sparks fell causing the brushwood to catch fire around his legs and immediately the living earth started to recede from him. As soon as he could, Arthur jumped over the flames to the larger rocks behind him and so made his escape to his horse.

"Not too bad at all," he said to his horse, "not too bad at all. Now, the Giant of the lake promised to lead us from the forest so let's see what happens."

He mounted his horse and looked around him. The fire still burning on the shore, shot out along the ground and over the rocks to where the horse and rider now waited. The animal showed no fear and Arthur kept absolutely still. The fire took a single line down a pathway.

"We follow the ribbon of fire," Arthur encouraged his horse. After a few yards the ribbon left the path and darted into the darkest part of the forest. "Let's proceed," Arthur gently instructed the horse. The fire turned this way and that way and eventually extinguished itself as Arthur rode from the Wandering Wood onto a fertile, green plain. He glanced back at the forest as he prepared to ride on and shouted, "I'll return."

At first there was silence and then a deep, eerie, gruff voice replied,

"I know you will, Arthur, King of the Celts and the lands beyond."

Arthur's task was clear. He had to discover within seven days the answer to the question posed by the Chieftain of the lake. It seemed a ridiculous task as the answer could be any number of things. But how could he, as a man, know what a woman wants more than anything and if he did find out from a woman, how would he know either that a particular woman was speaking for her whole sex or even if she was, whether the Chieftain would accept the answer? As a man, Arthur knew he might presume an answer which itself was completely wrong. In any case, could there be a right or a wrong answer? The whole matter was foolish. Why didn't the Chieftain merely fight with him? Why did he have to test him in terms of words and honour, whatever they meant? These thoughts were in his mind as he came to a river and saw a number of women washing clothes. He rode up to them and explained that he needed an answer to a question puzzling him. They willingly agreed to help him and so he asked them the question about what they wanted more than anything else in the world. One immediately answered, not to wash clothes day in and day out and they all laughed. Another said that she'd like a horse as beautiful as the stranger's, another talked of money, another talked of a faithful husband, another of a good lover. This sparked off a number of bawdy answers which had everyone laughing including Arthur. In the end, however, none of them could agree and so Arthur thanked them and continued on his way.

Arthur decided against going to the Northern fort near Cadair Idris but rather to plot a course from the River Tywi to the River Teifi and back again which he reckoned would take him the seven days. As he journeyed he visited a number of small settlements where the people recognised him as a great man because of his clothes and the horse he rode, but they didn't realise that they were speaking to their King nor did he reveal his identity but rather he merely explained his quest and asked his question. The answers were as numerous as the stars. Some wished for everlasting beauty or eternal youth, many wished for honest husbands, some for true love, some were longing to bear a child. Others wished that their children should be strong and healthy, one wished that her brother should return safely from King Arthur's camp. Arthur asked the name of the man, "Berne," came the reply and Arthur knew the man well since Berne had fought alongside him and had proved himself loyal. So Arthur resolved that when he reached his fort, he would send Berne home to his village for a month. One woman said she'd like to meet the King and Queen. At this Arthur laughed and the woman became embarrassed. Her name was Mai, the Welsh for May. The King resolved that she should be sent for on his return to help his wife.

He was overcome by the honesty of the people whom he met and silently thanked the Chieftain of the lake for freeing him to speak to so many of his own people and he felt humbled by their sincerity. These were the people for whom he fought. They were his people and he loved them. Nonetheless, they did not have the answer to his question which would satisfy him and therefore would not content the Chieftain. He had one day left and was journeying back to the forest when he saw a woman dressed in scarlet who was horribly disfigured. Her face was eaten away with a leprosy, her back was bent double and her bowed legs only just allowed her to hobble along the pathway. She reminded him of Morgen the witch, but there was no stench of evil around her only the deformity that she endured. Arthur rode up to her and although he wished her a good day, decided to ride immediately past her. As he did so, she called out, "Why don't you stop and talk to me? Am I not good enough for the likes of you?"

Arthur's heart sank. He felt chastened and pulled on the rein of the horse coming to a halt. He turned round and looked back at her.

"Is it because I'm so disfigured?" the woman asked.

Arthur wanted to deny the truth but he would not, so shamefully he confessed, "You know that it is and I am sorry."

The old woman tried to smile. "You are a good man," she said with surprise, "many would have whipped me as they rode by. I have the scars on my back to prove it. Do you want to see?"

"No, of course not, what can I do for you?" Arthur asked offering her some wine from his flask which she refused.

"I want you to treat me with respect."

"How do you mean?"

"You are a man on a quest," she continued, "I suggest you are an important man. For all I know, you could be King Arthur himself, our great ruler of this little world."

"And if I were?"

"If you were, if you are, why not ask me the question that you've been asking all the women you've met from the Tywi to the Teifi and back again?"

"You know that I am the King, don't you?"

"Yes," she answered.

"I apologise for the way I rode past you," Arthur said as he dismounted from his horse and came up to the old woman holding out his hand which she took.

"You are a wise woman," he continued, "and an honest one and I should have treated you better but I'll send doctors to you to see if they can cure you."

"Doctors," she sniffed, "no need. My cure lies in your hands."

"Tell me what I must do," King Arthur insisted, "and I'll help you. I promise."

"Simply ask me your question," she replied, "and then if I answer it to your satisfaction and that of the one to whom you are bound for an answer, promise to grant me whatever I wish."

King Arthur looked at her with sorrow and compassion. He wanted to help the woman if he could but how would she satisfactorily answer his question? "If it's in my power," he agreed.

"Then ask."

"Tell me," he paused, "tell me what is it that a woman wants more than anything else in the world?"

"Do you, Arthur our King, not know," the deformed woman mockingly asked repeating, "do you not know?" and then she laughed.

"I do not," the King confessed.

"Then, listen to me," the old woman commanded. She paused, looking into his eyes and said slowly, "Every woman wishes the same as every man. She wishes to have the freedom to be herself. The freedom, that is, to be who she is."

"And is that true?" the King enquired.

"It is as true as the deformity that you see before you."

Arthur thought for a while looking down towards where the River Tywi flowed past the forest where he was to return. "Thank you," he said. "Now I made you a promise, tell me what I need to do."

"If the lake Chieftain, whom I know sent you on this quest, is satisfied with the answer, meet me tomorrow evening at the edge of the forest and take me back to your fort. There I want to marry one of your warriors who must be strong and handsome."

"But," the King questioned, "will not marrying you, take away his freedom?"

"Only if he is forced to marry me, if he chooses to do so, he will gain his freedom and I will gain mine."

"What is your name?"

"What my name is does not matter and is of no consequence to you, but you can call me Gwen."

"Then, Gwen, by the promise I made to you, I will take your answer to the Chieftain of the lake and if he accepts it as true, I will meet you at the edge of the forest before the sun sets tomorrow and take you to my fort to be married."

"Thank you," she replied. "Now get on your way."

Arthur mounted his horse and leaving the woman he rode directly to the forest and followed a path. He knew it didn't matter which one since all led to the lake and soon he arrived at the rocks by the shore and tethered his horse. He did not venture onto the shore itself but remained on the rocks, climbing onto one of the great boulders. His golden hair hung down over his jerkin but as he prepared to shout out his arrival to the Chieftain, he noticed a young deer emerge from the water on the far side of the lake and run as fast as it could into the forest. After a moment, a yellow mist gathered on the surface of the water and a ghostly breeze collected itself and pursued the deer. The mist kept close to the ground and then as suddenly as it had appeared, it returned to the shore and spread across the lake where seeming to merge with the water, it disappeared.

Arthur again prepared to call out to the Chieftain but there was no need since he felt a wet, giant hand press against his shoulder.

"So you've returned," the Chieftain said as Arthur turned to be confronted by the ugly, pebbled face.

"I have."

"I knew you would, since you are not like the others. They leave the wood and run. They think that they can escape from me but they cannot. Breaches of trust, distractions from truth, hypocrisy can have only one result. They are found wanting in conscience and as cowards they die as surely as that young deer you watched has died."

"Why?"

"The traitors or the deer?"

"The deer."

"Because it did not ask my leave to bathe in my lake."

"That seems a little harsh," Arthur impishly replied.

The Chieftain laughed, "Arthur, I see what they tell me about you is true. Your innocence and naivety is to bring about a new way of thinking and maybe it already has. From this age through all ages, you will be known for your honesty and your bravery. I wish I had been the one to have it but you were chosen."

"I was," Arthur confirmed quietly repeating, "I was," as he thought briefly of that day he had been commissioned.

"I know," the Chieftain continued, "I saw you speak with Idris when at the summit of the mountain, he gave you his authority. Even from here I saw you and realised that I was not to be the one. Later, I saw him with his four daughters circle the sun and I knew how the end of this place would be. You were at the start of that end and from that time, I have lived a life of curse and cruelty waiting for my death or for yours. So now, my petulant King, tell me what it is to be, my life or yours?"

"You mean to fight with me?" Arthur asked adding as he placed his hand to his sword. "Then I am ready."

"No, no," the Chieftain insisted, "you do not understand. Whether you like it or not, you will die by the vapours that come from my lake unless I help you."

"And how can you do that?"

"By not allowing you to stay here for long enough for your lungs to be engulfed by them."

"So!"

"So, like, like, so. Arthur, you are a man of little words but tell me quickly the answer to my question. What does a woman desire above all else?"

"It isn't a difficult question to answer since a woman is no different from a man in her mind, will and spirit."

"What do you mean?" the Chieftain demanded abruptly.

"I mean that every woman wishes the same as every man. She wishes to have the freedom to be herself. The freedom, that is, to be who she is."

The Chieftain was silent and looked at Arthur intensely until eventually he asked, "Who has told you this?"

Arthur wondered whether to answer. "This is not part of the bargain," he ventured, "why should I tell you that?"

"Because the answer is the correct one and by it you have taken power away from me. There is no need for you to tell me your informant. It was Gwen, the deformed witch, my sister who from the moment of her birth was destined to bring about my destruction. Arthur, you are free to ride from this forest. Whenever you wish to leave, now and evermore, the ribbon of fire will appear to guide your way, but as for me, I am as a dead man. I will never see my lake purified, though one day you will fly high above it when a young woman will give it the purity of herself and cleanse it for ever. Watch, Arthur, watch my demise and tell Gwen, the cripple, that her task is done."

With that the Chieftain left Arthur and went to the side of the lake. He plunged into the water and swam out across its centre to the far shore. He then stood opposite on some rocks, facing Arthur. A yellowness gathered over the lake and came together in a mist. It rapidly moved across the far beach and over the rocks till it reached the Chieftain's feet. It swirled round him, making a tightening gyre around his legs, his groin, his waist, his chest, his arms, his neck and finally his head. The Giant toppled from the rocks to the shore, the mist enveloping him. Then as suddenly as it had all begun, the mist left the body and rushed back into the lake. The live earth took its share of the spoils and the Chieftain's remains were devoured by the growing clay. Arthur saw it all. When the stillness came, there was nothing more to be seen. Arthur waited in silence and with sadness untethered his horse, mounted it and looked for his path out of the Wandering Wood. The ribbon of fire appeared which he followed until he reached the edge of the forest where Gwen was waiting for him.

"Is it over?" she asked.

"It's over."

"He is dead then?"

"Yes."

"He was my brother."

"I know."

"We were both cursed."

"He told me that you were."

"No, both of us were cursed but didn't he tell you that the curse could only be lifted by the death of one of us? He died for me. You thought he was cruel, but he was kind. He knew that only King Arthur could endure the smell and stench of that place until the time is right for it to be cleansed. He anticipated your coming, conjured the paths, made his plans and waited for you to carry out his wishes, as did I, and so he died for me to give me a life."

"I will enquire no further," Arthur said, "except whether you still intend to travel with me and marry one of my warriors, my knights."

"I do," came the swift reply.

Arthur dismounted from his horse and said, "Then, Gwen, let me help you onto my horse. If you allow me, I will ride with you since my horse will bear the weight of us both."

"Thank you, Sir," Gwen answered politely, "please help me up to my place."

Arthur did so and then mounted the horse himself and the two of them made their way to the Southern camp, Arthur not having even seen the mountain to which he had intended to go or his Northern camp beyond it.

They rode for three days stopping each day as the light faded at which time Gwen hurried away from the King to ensure her privacy only to reappear the next morning after dawn to continue their journey. It was, however, in the afternoon of the third day that Gwen saw the hillside fort in the distance.

"Sir," she said, "please take me only as far as the settlement below the hill. You enter the camp and once one of your warriors has agreed to marry someone as loathsome in looks as me, fly a red flag. I will enter and make my way directly to the place where I will be married. There I will meet my husband at twelve noon and we will be married immediately, if that is, I like him. If I do not, you will have betrayed me."

"I don't recall," Arthur responded quickly, "that whether you like him or not was part of the bargain."

She cackled. "If he is one of your bravest warriors, strong and handsome, I will like him. That was the bargain."

"So it was," Arthur agreed adding quietly to himself that the words would be hard to realise.

They rode to one of the farming settlements at the foot of the Southern fort and there the deformed woman dismounted from the horse and hobbled off into the crowds buying and selling at a market. There was a great deal of activity and Arthur soon lost sight of her even clothed as she was in her scarlet dress. He prodded his horse and up the hill they rode towards the fort. He felt leaden, weighed down with what he had to do. How could he ask one of his companions to marry such a thing as had ridden with him? It was clear that she was courteous and gentle but for a young warrior to have such deformity for a wife was very hard. It was unfair on the individual and on him as King having to impose such a demand on one of his followers. Yet he had made a promise and words are all that we have to go on.

A crowd of people came out to see their King enter his fort. Normally on his return, he'd make a fuss of everyone but not this time. He sent a message that his warriors and Merlin must meet with him immediately in the great hall as there was something of utmost importance to be decided.

Arthur went to refresh himself before speaking briefly with the Queen and then made his way to the hall where the warriors had assembled as instructed. By the time he arrived, therefore, everyone was in place to greet their returning King. Merlin welcomed him back asking everyone for calm heads and clear thinking in all that needed to be decided. Then there was silence.

Merlin eventually broke the tension by asking the King politely what they were to discuss. Arthur paused and then stated, "Marriage." The knights looked at each other perplexed as this wasn't a normal topic for discussion. He fell silent again then eventually rose to his feet and announced, "Friends, I have done one of you a great disservice."

"Never!" Gawain exclaimed.

"Yes I have, my friend, and I will tell you how."

With that the King told his whole story, accurately and truthfully, concluding as he looked towards Merlin with the question, "So what is to be done?"

"It is difficult to say," Merlin began, "very difficult, but clearly…" he continued but was interrupted by Gawain who stated quite categorically, "There is nothing difficult about it. I will not have my King embarrassed or humiliated. He had to make this bargain because had he not, he would have been killed and we would have lost our leader. The bargain was a blind one made to a woman whom he pitied. Perhaps she should have shown pity in return but apparently she did not. The King cannot marry her himself since he is not one of his own warriors and besides, he is already married and our new law does not allow us to be married to two women at the same time. Is that not so, Merlin?"

Merlin nodded his agreement, since this had been a matter of much debate in the country and had caused significant unease and even resentment.

"Then the answer is simple," Gawain continued. "No one else has offered this woman marriage, so I will. I, Gawain, will marry the deformed Gwen. Let the red flag be flown."

"My Lord...," Merlin protested.

"No argument, Merlin my friend. She entered into an agreement with the King so I love Gwen for all her deformity. She has pluck and she's after respectability and a husband which is what all women want. I'll give her both."

"It's not what she says all women desire," the King corrected him.

"No matter," Gawain argued, "it's what she desires or she'd have never made such a bargain. Please, Sir, allow me to marry her. I want to marry her."

All in the room were stunned. The King withdrew for a discussion with Merlin and when they returned he said, "Be it as Gawain wishes. Raise the red flag and at noon tomorrow, gather in the chapel and let all my warriors witness Gawain's marriage to Gwen. In the meantime, everyone is to disperse except for Berne with whom I wish to speak."

The King took Berne aside and instructed him that he should travel to his village to visit his family and that every year he was to spend a month with them as they missed him so much. Berne readily agreed since he too missed his sisters, brothers and his parents. Arthur was pleased and told Berne that he should leave after Gawain's wedding the following day. The King then went to see the Queen and told her about Mai, whose honesty had so impressed him. Guinevere agreed that Mai should work with her and messengers were sent to the village to bring the young woman to the fort. Arthur was a man without comparison, he was as written, "the once and future King."

It is difficult to imagine what thoughts went through Gawain's mind that night. Had he been too impetuous?

Would the woman he was to marry be as horrendous as the King had described? He was sure that she would be since he had never known the King to tell a lie. How would he spend his life with such a one? Was he to be the butt of jokes or was he to be pitied and patronised as no doubt this woman was day in and day out. There was no resolution to the problem, he had agreed to marry her and so he would. He had to trust to fate that all would be well. He kept all these concerns to himself and his companions didn't speak of the matter, not with him at least. They showed respect to a man whom they loved but whom they considered to be foolhardy. The King was beside himself with grief, speaking with Merlin and Guinevere but neither could offer any consolation to him. What else could he have done? He went over the events of the forest, time and time again. He had been trapped by circumstances as surely as the old woman was trapped in her deformity. Guinevere tried to comfort him but he couldn't sleep.

The next day the whole of the camp assembled in the chapel before noon. The deformed woman had set out hobbling her way towards the fort. The King sent a rider out to help her but she refused any assistance and stubbornly made her way on foot. The rider returned to confirm that the description that the King had given of this woman was true. She was hideous in her deformity.

Eventually, when Gwen arrived, the little girl who had been chosen to present her with a posy of flowers, refused to do so bursting into tears at the sight of the woman whilst some youngsters sniggered and many of the serving women cried. Others merely remained silent as Gwen made her way to the wedding. Gawain standing before Merlin had his back to the door and heard the gasp of the assembly and the exclamations of grief from his friends. Turning he saw the diminutive figure waiting at the door alone but seeing beyond her deformity, to a person of feelings and fears, he strode up to her calling out, "Why has my Gwen no flowers?"

Someone came forward from the crowd outside with the posy and gave it to Gawain. The warrior-knight then, in full view of all, knelt before Gwen and offered her the flowers. "Lady," he said, "take these from the man who wishes to marry you."

Gwen accepted the flowers, attempted to smile signalling to Gawain to get to his feet. The King and Queen watched as Gawain kissed Gwen on her cheek and then gallantly led her towards Merlin.

"Who gives this woman in marriage?" Merlin asked.

"I do," replied the King, "if she is happy with the man who wishes to marry her."

"I am happy," Gwen confirmed. "I am happy with him and with the courtesy you have shown me, Arthur, King of these lands."

So it was that Gawain married Gwen. There were many at the wedding, however, who did not share the knights' magnanimity or the King's. They were cross about what had happened and though at the wedding feast they danced and drank and ate well, they muttered behind the King's back that he had wronged a brave and handsome warrior. Gwen did not eat or drink nor did she attempt to dance. She appeared bemused by everything that had happened until early in the evening, before darkness drew in, she made her excuses and went to her room, asking Gawain to follow later.

Gawain didn't drink or eat much either. He felt sick by what had happened confiding only in Merlin who told him that the doctors might be able to straighten the woman's back and heal the sores on her face. It would take time, perhaps many years, but possibly something could be done at least to help her.

The young knight then went to his quarters to find Gwen sitting in front of a mirror, with her back to him.

"Gawain," she asked, "are you ready for our wedding night?"

"I am."

"Then," she said, "look at your bride."

With that turning to face her husband the most beautiful woman Gawain had ever seen stood up before him. Gawain gasped not knowing what to say. Gwen was young and graceful, everything that he had dreamed of. It was as if all his longings were as one.

"What is this?" he stammered.

"I am cursed," she explained. "For half of every day, I am deformed and for half of any day I am as beautiful as you see me now. What do you say?"

"I say that we find a way to lift the curse and gain your beauty for the whole of every day."

Gwen laughed. "I can do that by briefly disguising my beauty as a deformity as I sometimes did when I was with the King but I cannot hide my deformity as beauty. No, that is not the answer, but you can help since you have a choice. You can decide whether I am to be beautiful for you at night or beautiful for you during the day. You cannot sleep in my bed until the choice has been made."

Gawain thought and then said, "By night."

"What a selfish man you are," she replied. "Do you not want me to have the dignity and respectability of my beauty during the day when I appear at your side? Do you just wish to possess my beauty as a selfish desire, allowing me no freedom? This is the wrong answer."

"I'm sorry," Gawain apologised. "Forgive me. Keep your beauty for the day."

"Is that how you insult me, you do not wish to enjoy my beauty in the privacy of our own bedroom? You'd rather, in your pride, merely show me off as a beauty to the other warrior-knights, to the gossips and the servants, nothing more than a selfish possession? This is the wrong answer."

"I'm sorry, but I don't know how to answer. If I say by night, then I'm wrong. If I say during the day, I'm wrong. You must decide for yourself, you must be who you are. You must be free to be yourself as and when you want."

"Oh Gawain," she joyfully cried out. "You have lifted the curse placed on me and my brother over whom King Arthur triumphed in the woods by the lake. By your words I am free to be myself and that is what I will be. My deformity has gone for ever and I remain your wife."

They went to embrace but Gawain held back.

"And is this why you married me?" he asked.

"It is."

"And would you have married me, Gwen, if the curse had not made you so desperate as to find someone like me to help you?"

"I can't tell."

Gawain thought, turning things over and over in his mind before saying, "Gwen, you've just attained the freedom that has evaded you since the curse was placed on you. Don't doubt that I am distracted by your beauty, by your honesty and by the grace you have shown to me in choosing me to be the one to set you free. But I will not take advantage of you. We are not finally married until we have consummated our vows. That we must not do since such an act would take away the freedom which you have never enjoyed.

I would not do that to you for all the gold in the hills beside the River Mawddach."

Gwen smiled at him and replied, "Gawain, your courtesy and kindness is beyond anything I have known throughout my life. You are offering me my freedom and it is an offer which I accept because it is generously given by such a man as you."

With that Gawain and Gwen went to see Merlin and explained all that had occurred. Merlin spoke with the King who laid his hands on the couple. Arthur ordered that a horse was to be given to Gwen for her journey the following day. Gwen spent the night alone and alone as beautiful as in the night, she left the camp at dawn. From their room the Queen and King Arthur watched her leave.

"Where will she go?" the Queen wondered.

"To her home," the King replied.

"And where is that?"

"I didn't think it important to ask," he told her, adding, "nor did Gawain."

FOUR
RHITA GAWR

How can a giant of a man be small in stature? Arthur was a giant in his bravery but he fought as a man against the tallest of all giants, Rhita Gawr.

Rhita Gawr was a colossus of evil, as fearful as you can imagine. He was the tallest of all giants and he roamed the country from the Northern arm of the land jutting out into the sea, down to the great mountain, Idris' throne. Rhita was known as the "unassailable," as no one could defeat him. Warriors from all over the land, from the hills, from the Saxon invaders, from Celtic Ireland and the great lands to the South, from Scotland, from over the seas and the lands far away, came to challenge Rhita Gawr. He pressed them to death with his shield; he sliced them in two with his sword; he strangled them with his bare hands. They were all destroyed by the Giant whom no one could defeat. Rhita was not just tall, but weirdly evil since once he killed his foe, he would take out his knife and cut off the beard of his victim. He would then boil the flesh and eat it and make a liquor from the blood. The beard he would sew on to his cloak so that all would see his greatness in victory. So many had he killed and devoured that his whole cloak had become as a single beard from collar to foot. It was as

Merlin once said, "a fabrication from the trophies of his carnage." And so Rhita Gawr would appear as a grizzled beard, tall as the sky, terrible as the wind, cold as the snow, showing neither mercy nor kindness. He scavenged the land and ate man and beast, woman and child so that he became a curse to the homelands from where people already fleeing from the Saxons now fled to the hills to avoid the evil giant and there they prayed that someone would come to protect and release them all from Rhita Gawr.

It was in the midsummer that Arthur had arrived at the plains of Cadair where the River Mawddach ebbs and flows according to the motions of the tide. There he harnessed his horse and ascended the mountain with Merlin as his guide. It was good to climb the steep slopes again where years before he had taken his commission from Idris the god. The air was fresh and from the mountain side they could see the curves of the land, cradling the bright blue bay that is the source of the rain and the water in the streams. At one time, the dolphins jumped in that bay, but no more. Perhaps they had taken refuge near the islands, swimming in the sea beyond, but it was nevertheless tranquillity itself that day and Merlin felt contented in Arthur's company despite the stories of the man-eater, the beard-coated Giant. When they had almost reached the top of Cadair's ridge, they were seen. From far off beyond the Rhinog mountain and the round backed hill called Moelfre, Rhita Gawr had received news of the prize he longed for, the golden beard of Arthur. The King, by this time, had reached the summit admiring the views over the bright blue bay and out to the sea which separates Wales from Ireland. But as he talked to Merlin of the beauty of the sight, the mountain reverberated with the sound of the Giant's cry.

"What are you and who are you that dare climb my mountain and cross my lands?"

Arthur smiled at Merlin putting his finger to his lips and made no reply. Furious the Giant roared again, "Why do you not answer me? What are you and who are you that dare climb my mountain and cross my lands?"

The King still made no reply.

"Curse your impudence," roared the Giant, "what are you, I demand to know, and who are you that dare climb my mountain and cross my lands?"

Arthur ignoring the wild shouts sat down and staring out to the sea said to Merlin, "My dear friend, is not this land a place of great beauty, where the green hills roll down to the plains and onwards to the bay and yet, in places, sheer down into a rocky cliff falling into the sea itself?" He paused deep in thought before continuing, "I remember, my Merlin, that the dolphins used to jump in the bright blue water of the bay. Where have they gone…?"

The King was interrupted with a further yell that, in its ferocity, had even mighty Cadair Idris shaking so much that boulders rolled downwards towards the estuary. At this with a wink at Merlin, Arthur rose to his feet again and assumed a stature as tall as Rhita Gawr himself. He became so tall, mighty and powerful that it was as if he were Idris the god. Merlin was aghast to see him and yet proud to look at his King, his master whose golden hair was blowing in the breeze of Cadair. "Oh my King, my Arthur, my pupil, you are as a god, a giant as tall as Rhita himself." Arthur stood on the summit of Cadair and stared across to where Rhita prowled the hillside further to the North but who was silenced by the miraculous apparition of the King. Nevertheless he now stood his ground waiting for Arthur to reply as did all the people of the oppressed land and even Merlin himself. Everyone waited for King Arthur to speak and when he did, all listened.

"Rhita Gawr," the King began in an authoritative voice which could be heard across all the land, "I am Arthur, King of the Celts, Lord of this island and the lands beyond and I am here to fight and destroy you, to free the people and restore this land over which I am the rightful King."

"Arthur, King of Nowhere," retorted Gawr, "I have waited for this day, for your flesh will make a midsummer banquet for me. That Arthur should come to me for his death is something which I have longed for. Not only your beard will I have, but your golden hair for my belt."

"And so you may," replied the King, "but only in your dreams. So dream and dream man-eater. Dream on until your death at my hands. Look, look across the bay for by the end of today, there your beard will float in the sea whilst your body will be taken to raise a snow capped mountain, whose peak I will enjoy seeing from this Throne of Idris bequeathed to me for ever."

"Contemptible boy," the Giant raged, "come down from my footstool and meet me on the plain below."

King Arthur raised his head to the heavens as if to commune with Idris himself before looking again at the Giant he solemnly said, "Rhita Gawr, prepare for death. King Arthur comes."

Merlin reports that there was such majesty, such authority, such brave determination in the King's pronouncement that there was no doubt of his victory. This was Arthur, the appointed King, the proclaimed ruler of the people. There was no other. The evil would surely be overcome but as Arthur regained his normal stature and descended the hills with Merlin, the Giant's footsteps were heard making their way to the estuary below them. Gradually the sun itself was hidden as the shadow of Rhita Gawr covered the land. Merlin's initial confidence, he later admitted, allowed some fear, only a little but some since Rhita Gawr was a prodigious monster. Merlin asked Arthur whether he was going to transform himself once more into a giant in order to fight the evil before him but Arthur shook his head saying, "Merlin, my friend, I am but a man as you are. That Idris gave me a stature on the mountain was his affair only to show his glory in me but no I fight as he wishes, as the thing that I am, a man of flesh and blood and a servant of the god through whom I have my authority."

As Arthur continued down the mountain he used the natural echo of the land to distract the Giant. Shouting this way and that so first appearing to be in one place and then in another, on top of the mountain or below it, to one side or another. The Giant kept surveying the terrain to ascertain where the two men were but they were invisible in the trees, shrubs and bracken on the mountain side. Birds, silent for many years in the presence of Rhita Gawr, began to sing once more and the bees came alive in the heather providing the hum of nature. As if inspired, Arthur himself began to sing, the song reverberating across the valley to torment Gawr,

"Rhita Gawr, Rhita Gawr, forbear to tread much further
The river so long is mighty and wide,
It twists and swirls, twists and divides.
The water fills from the mighty sea
And your coat will be your despair,
Your coat will be your despair."

The Giant took no notice of the words and the light began to return as the sun rose higher. King Arthur, meanwhile, having descended Cadair had untethered his horse, riding it midway down the valley to where the gold mines are. His horse, named Marchwyn, was pure white like the fresh snow from which a further mountain claimed its name. The horse, however, had a mind of its own and drawn by something glinting in the sun took Arthur to the entrance of one of the gold mines. There deep underground, the people of the land had made for their King, whom they were sure would come to free them, a suit of pure gold which they called his armour. This, along with a sturdy shield and a long, golden lance had been laid out for him to wear and use though the people were nowhere to be seen. Arthur blessed them for their kindness as Merlin caught up with his King and helped him prepare for battle. The armour fitted the King exactly and glistening and shining in the sunlight, Arthur remounted Marchwyn who proudly, despite the extra weight, galloped from the mine.

The Giant needed no horse since he stood the height of horse and man and much more. When Rhita Gawr saw Arthur at last, he charged at him with a deafening yell running full pelt along the valley. Arthur was as determined as the day when tied to a rock he had been whipped and tortured by Morgen. But today she was not to be seen only the towering frame of Gawr bearing down on him, lashing out with a mighty axe which, beyond belief, the King parried with the new shield he carried. Rhita Gawr turned and charged again but Arthur's horse stood its ground, its master in control. Again and again Arthur parried every blow, the shield glinting in the sun. Each time he parried, Arthur appeared to grow in confidence as his foe diminished.

The Giant decided that his axe would not prevail, not even against his longed for enemy. Instead he would press the King to death with his shield and charged once more at Arthur. This time as he reached the King, he threw down his weapon and swiftly grasping his shield in both hands, he fell forward, onto Arthur knocking him from Marchwyn.

As he fell, Arthur firmly grasped the sword he had once released from the stone to attack but found that even that could not pierce the Giant's shield. Arthur landed in the watery sand still gripping the sword which did not buckle as the prodigious weight of Rhita Gawr and his shield now fell upon it. The sand, however, began to give way under such weight and the Giant and Arthur slowly started to sink within it. Merlin feared for the King. Would he drown in the fearful muddy flats of the Mawddach? "On, Arthur," he cried, "you have the strength, you have the strength."

Did Arthur hear him? It does not matter for the King was born to survive, he had to survive. As he sank, he found a rescue since beneath the sands was lodged a large boulder which gave the King the platform he needed for his back. With this firmness behind him, he put all his strength into the hilt of his sword and determinedly pushed the mighty weight of Rhita Gawr and his shield upwards and upwards. With heaves and shouts of pain, Arthur lifted himself to his feet, thrusting the Giant backwards. Rhita Gawr, however, did not fall. In being thrown back he regained his feet on the Mawddach flats and stooped for his axe. Idris' daughter, Morwen of the Sea, now showed her support of King Arthur as the tide turned and the sea waters started to seep back above and below the sand and mud and over the mudflats. It was now the Giant's turn to experience the loss of ground. His weight dragged him down into the watery sand so that his feet became heavy with wetness and the cloggy ripples of the mud beneath. His giant stature had turned against him and would have likewise turned against the King if he had decided to fight as a giant rather than as a man. Then Rhita Gawr's bearded coat became saturated with the tidal water flowing back up the estuary from the sea. As the water lapped against the first beard, a wonder occurred never to be seen or heard again. The beard coat acquired a voice as the spirit of one of the beards of a dead warrior returned to it, "Arthur, Arthur," this voice cried, "you come to avenge."

"And so I do," shouted the King. Then as if awakened by the first beard, the second and the third, the fourth and the fifth, the sixth and the seventh acquired their voices as did the eighth and the ninth and the tenth and then all so that the great Giant's coat cried with one voice, filling the valley with its horror, "Rhita Gawr, Rhita Gawr, you will be slain, you will be dead for ever. The King of all earthly kings has come to take your beard and with it, your life. Rhita Gawr you will despair and be killed, despair at your death, despair and be damned for ever. Despair Rhita Gawr. Despair. Despair. Your death has come."

At this the Giant grasping his axe from the waters weaved his axe back and forth, slashing at the beards with it but the axe was deflected by the bristles which had become taut and harder than any metal known to living man. He threw the weapon from him once more and drew his sword but to no avail, it could do no better than the axe in the Giant's attempt to dislodge the beards from his grizzly coat. With every movement of the Giant the beards cried louder, "Rhita Gawr, Rhita Gawr, you are dying, despair and be damned for ever, damned for ever, damned for ever!"

The frenzied Giant went into a panic as hurling his now useless sword into the water he tried to unbuckle his coat. Meanwhile Arthur waiting, thanking silently the souls of the dead for their assistance, saw his advantage in this great event. He remounted his horse, which all this time had stood patiently even as the ever deepening water lapped around its legs, and with the battle cry, "I am Arthur, King of the Celts and the lands beyond," he charged at Rhita Gawr.

The Giant bent low to regain his sword but the beards raged their taunts, "You are dead, you are dead, you are dead," but seemingly to the watching Merlin, to no end as Rhita Gawr stood so tall. The Giant, however, in retrieving his sword from the waters found that his feet were so entrenched in the mud that he could scarcely move. Still he raised the mighty sword high into the sky to kill his foe. If he brought it down upon Arthur, nothing could save the King since the Giant would have sliced through Arthur's livery, his golden armour, his strong limbs and his white horse with one blow. Arthur's great sword, though long, was not of a length to do what Arthur needed. But at the side of his horse, Arthur carried the golden lance given to him by the people of the mines. Sheathing the sword he held the lance firmly with both hands. The Giant was to suffer a lesson of his own. Rhita Gawr, with all his giant strength behind it, brought down his sword towards Arthur and with it the prodigious weight of his enormous body. But Arthur tightening his grip on the people's weapon, raised the lance upwards towards the Giant's chest. His timing was faultless. Rhita Gawr was impaled through the momentum of his own downward thrust, the golden lance entering Gawr's chest exposed by the unbuttoning of his grizzled jacket. The lance plunged deep through his ribs towards the foul heart of the foul fiend, pushing the Giant back onto his feet. At that there was a mighty cheer from the spirits of the morbid coat that the Giant had worn and from Merlin, as he watched from the bank of the river. Arthur, now glorious once more in his attire, charged past the wounded Gawr towards the sun. The lance remained where it struck and Arthur looking back saw it pulsating, sending a gruesome jolting shadow across the waters. Blood poured in torrents from the wound that the King had inflicted. The beards, which at first had cried out in joy at Arthur's charge, now became eerily silent as the Giant still standing turned towards Arthur. They had fought and battled each other throughout the afternoon and the long evening but as the sun sunk low over the sea behind the King, it dazzled and blinded Rhita Gawr. The Giant went to lift his sword but slowly fell to his knees, discarding his weapon into the Mawddach as now with his huge hands, he grasped the throbbing lance attempting to remove it from his chest.

Arthur, his back to the sea and sun, rode towards the dying Giant and dismounted from his horse into the water which for him was now chest high. With one voice, the beards cried afresh, "Arthur, King of the Celts and the land beyond, set us free, set us free, set us free."

"I will," confirmed the King.

At this, the Giant dropped from his knees into the grim water with such ferocity that the fall sent the water in the river back towards the sea. Arthur had to act fast since he saw out in the bay a gathering wave, climbing as the outgoing water met the incoming tide. This bore-like wave would surely come and overwhelm them all. From the bank, Merlin prayed for the King who was facing this unexpected danger.

"Be quick, be quick, kill him and free yourself," the beards cried. "Free us, free us and protect yourself."

Arthur took his mighty sword and as the approaching wave from the sea journeyed up the river, sliced off the beard of the Giant, Rhita Gawr, making him no more than his victims of the past. At that there was a loud sigh from the coat of beards as the souls of the victims were released. The air resounded with words rippling in a crescendo of noise across the water towards Cadair Idris, "We are avenged by Arthur our King." The great mountain echoed the name of "Arthur, Arthur, Arthur," so that the whole valley seemed to be triumphantly crying out the King's name. Arthur, who was just a man, became distracted feeling proud of what he'd done and of the sound of his name reverberating up and down the estuary. But the danger was not over as life had not totally drained from the Giant. Rhita still had some strength left in his arm and as Arthur went to remount his horse listening to his name echoing around Cadair, Rhita Gawr grabbed him pulling him away from Marchwyn.

"King of Nowhere," gasped the expiring Giant, "we will die together."

"Not so," replied the King holding high the shaved off beard, "for you will see your beard flow upon the great wave as it returns to the sea."

With that, the Giant and the King were overwhelmed by the approaching wave which drove past them and through them. Marchwyn was swept away, innocent last victim of the evil Gawr, but Arthur was still held in the grip of the Giant's hand. As the water swelled over them, the Giant's grip remained steadfast and irony upon irony saved the King from drowning. It was only in the aftermath of the wave, that the Giant, gasping for breath, released his hold. Arthur struggling free, fell into the remains of the swell being sucked under the ferocious water which ripped his armour from him. Merlin watched the wave raging further up the valley of the Mawddach towards Tabor Mountain and the Dinas Pass, Arthur's golden armour being taken with it still glinting in the dying sun as it surfaced in the water and disappeared again. Merlin turning back, could see no sign of the King. "Arthur, Arthur, my King, my Lord," he beseeched but there was only the silence of despair. He feared the worst, if the armour had succumbed so too may have the King. With tears in his eyes, he strained despairingly to see whether Arthur, in the end, had survived.

It was then that the departing spirits from the coat of Rhita Gawr hauntingly cried out from the mountain where they were gathering, "Come back, come back to life and to fame for ever, Arthur, King of the Celts, King of the Lands Beyond, King of the Island. Come back and live and endure your fame."

Merlin shuddered at the sound of these strange voices but as they called the King to come from the depths, Arthur rose out of the waters and with his magisterial presence, turned to the prostrate Giant and proclaimed, "Although you saved my life, now you must die. For see, your beard is on the wave which will return to overwhelm you."

With that Arthur swam to the shore whilst the tidal wave turned and rushed back down the river, the beard of Rhita Gawr at its crest. The Giant tried to rise as he reached out for his beard but he was hit by the water which raged down to the sea and out into the bay where the beard of Rhita Gawr floated in the sea just as Arthur had foreseen.

When all was calm again, Arthur swam back to where the Giant lay and ensured that Rhita Gawr was no more. The spirits of the beards in the air cried out, "Farewell, Arthur, great King. Farewell," their voices fading as if being absorbed into the great mountain until there was silence.

As Cadair Idris could not be desecrated nor the spirits of the Giant's victims defiled, the freed people of the land took away the body of Rhita Gawr and encased it in another mountain in the North. Stones were laid upon him raising the height of the mountain towards the sky. The spirits of his victims now at peace in Idris' mountain, their beards were strewn across the land as a reminder of all that had occurred. These beards petrified as they fell into a greyness of slate which still denotes the land to this day. It is said that the people then salvaged the golden armour and the lance they had given to the King and took them back into the caves for when King Arthur might need them again. But some claim that not all the armour was found and that fragments of it remain deeply buried in the river bed. King Arthur had come out of the water for a second time having been called by the dead, protected by the gods and the elements and helped by the living. He and Merlin held each other in triumph before climbing the mountain to give thanks to Idris and his four daughters who had witnessed it all. They then returned to their fort, cheered all along the way by the freed people of the newly liberated land.

FIVE

SIR GAWAIN AND THE GREEN KNIGHT

What happened that festive season as the New Year approached may have been instigated by Merlin or some may say, plotted by Morgen. Whatever, it was to prove one of the greatest adventures undertaken by any of Arthur's Knights. Did Arthur have a premonition about it? I cannot say. But during the festive season his mind was wracked with pain at the decline in the courageous activities of his warriors. He determined, therefore, to make an example of himself in order to shame his Knights into accepting their responsibilities. "Be not men of the night," he would say to them, "but Knights of the day."

As all gathered for the New Year's Eve celebrations in the great hall, Arthur appeared not in his robes of states or those for war, but in sackcloth, faithful Gafallt his dog at his side. His Knights and the whole camp were stunned into silence by the sight of their King. With Gafallt sitting back on his hind legs next to his master as loyal and alert as any dog could be, the King rebuked his warriors.

"Neither men of the night nor Knights of the day," he began. Looking round at them all with challenging contempt he continued, "During the last twelve months, I have seen no evidence of feats of arms by any of you, my companions. Not one adventure of note has been recorded in our fortress here or anywhere else. Not one of you has journeyed to Idris' mountain high above the Mawddach River to pay respects to my forebear. Our crops have shown signs of decline and at times this past summer, we have had days of endless rain so that the sun was hardly seen. All this has strengthened my resolve not to feast with you any more this season but to keep a fast until one of you, my Knights, recounts an adventure of worth and note that has occurred during this last year or until a new adventure begins. But this is my fast not yours and therefore, though I will not join in myself, the feasting should continue."

The King looked around the hall, no one spoke and neither did he. Instead he took his seat and signalled for a goblet of water. The unease remained, eyes fell and heads sank; silence prevailed, revealing despondency. Finally the King broke the tension by leaning down to Gafallt stroking him and playing with his ears. This informality gave Gawain the courage to speak up. "Sir, how can your vow be relieved since we know that no such adventure can be recounted and one is unlikely to begin during the festivities? It is too cold for fighting and simply not the season for adventure."

"Believe me, Gawain," the King sternly replied, "an adventure will either be recounted or begun this night for the glory of my people and my land or I will neither eat nor drink in this company. So, my friends, I will fast but you can be merry, eat your fill, satisfy your thirst and talk the time away. Tonight I know there will be an event of wonder. Be expectant. Trust me."

The King signalled to the servants to serve food and drink while he turned to Gafallt and played with him again.

Gradually people began to talk but how could they eat without guilt if the King refused to eat with them? Sir Kay stood up in an attempt to break the despondency in the room and told the story of Peredur coming to court. This was a simple narrative well known to everyone but it broke the ice. People began to eat and as Sir Kay spoke, they became more interested since Peredur himself was at the banquet that night. The story recounted how Peredur when he first arrived at the fort had been ridiculed by Kay as being a boy of no significance. He had no training, no skills, no weapon of any kind except sticks and stones. But the story was to turn against Sir Kay since Peredur left the fort and challenged a warrior whom they called Golden Ring because he kept circling around the camp's perimeter during sunlight challenging anyone to a fight. The boy fought him and won, piercing Golden Ring's eye with a wooden stick. It was listened to by everyone who appreciated Kay's own feeling of humiliation in the part he'd played in the tale of Peredur's anger and then of the young boy's remorse at the fact that he had killed a man. King Arthur, of course, had looked after the boy and had long since brought him into the fort as a warrior, resilient in his courage and appreciative of people's lives.

Throughout the telling of the tale, Arthur had listened attentively but everyone knew it to be an old tale not a new one as the King demanded. As the story came to an end, Gafallt barked and everyone sensed that something was wrong. The musicians were about to start playing but Gafallt barked again. The King patted him and looked to Merlin who rose from the table and rapped the floor with his staff. Gafallt barked for a third time with a canine intuition which seemed to bring a cold chill into the room and shed unease across the hall. Outside the wind raged through the trees, yet faintly, without doubt, the hooves of a horse could be heard galloping towards them. The wind gained in intensity as the horse approached and the oak doors rattled in their frames. Gafallt growled but was silenced with a look from the King who gave an order to the servants to raise the cross beam of the doors. He signalled to Owain to take his place at the head of the table. Quickly one of the servants brought out the King's best cloak and draped it around Owain. The King meanwhile, in his sackcloth, sat at the servants' end of the room. The doors secured now only by the great wooden latch shook with increased agitation. The wind howled as the galloping animal approached closer and closer to the assembled throng. As the horse's hooves clattered outside, anxious glances were exchanged in the hall. The warriors checked that their swords were ready for any emergency but they would take orders only from the King and Lancelot would lead them in any fight that might ensue. As the tension mounted, the shrill neighing of the horse seemed to surround them. Suddenly, the wind dropped and the sound of the horse disappeared with it. A taught silence ensued. Still King Arthur, Merlin, Lancelot, Kay, Owain, Gawain and the rest waited. After a pause that seemed like eternity, there was a horrendous noise as the doors of the great hall burst open. The moonlight streamed in revealing a grotesque figure, almost too disgusting to describe. It was filth itself. Slowly it rode its horse into the hall coming to a halt between the tables. Everyone was mesmerised. The massive animal was draped all in green but was itself all green. On it was seated a hideous warrior clothed all in green but who himself was all green. No one had seen anything like it before. It was a dirty green, a slimy green not the green of spring. The Knight's jerkin was green, his sleeves were green, his gloves were green, his flesh was green, his eyes were green; his green hair hung down almost to his waist and was cut round all in one length. There amidst them all horse and rider stood as still as a ship becalmed.

No one spoke, the tension could be cut. Not even the dogs barked, rather they cowered near the doorways except for Gafallt who had surreptitiously moved round to the entrance of the hall behind the Green Knight and had positioned himself looking challengingly at the monster in the middle of the room. If the Green Knight were to leave, he'd have to tackle the King's dog at least.

The Green Knight perused the assembly and focussed his eyes on Owain seated in the King's place. "Which of you," he enquired in a voice which was polite and courteous, "is the King?"

"I speak for him," Owain confidently replied.

"And so you may but you are not him," retorted the visitor with a smile. "You are Sir Owain and I have no business with you."

There was silence again as the Green Knight scratching his face with a twig of green holly, surveyed the company, first looking at the Knights and then at the servants until he focussed on the one in the sackcloth. He stared unflinchingly until Arthur smiling, authoritatively stepped forward saying, "Sir Knight, what would you have to do with me?"

"Now," replied the Knight, throwing the holly stick into the fire, "I speak with King Arthur, my greetings to you and to my old friend, Merlin, your Counsellor." Arthur looked towards Merlin and he in some amazement returned his glance. Merlin had no idea who this apparition might be as the Green Knight grinned, showing his dirty green teeth.

"King Arthur," he continued, "I know well that your warriors languish in the lasciviousness of the luxurious. For twelve months I have watched and seen no signs of gallantry. There have been no challenges, no trials of skills; there have been ceremonies, there have been quests but no feats of renown. Why is this? Is King Arthur's court fallacious in reputation?" The Knight looked around and added with a hint of contempt, "Is Arthur himself a vanquished King destroyed by his own ineptitude?" He turned his gaze from King Arthur towards Lancelot then to Owain and then Gawain before impudently adding, "I pause for a reply."

"What would you have to do with me?" the King repeated.

"King Arthur the impotent…," the Green Knight began but at this insult Lancelot, perhaps guiltily, made to draw his sword and Gafallt growled. The King signalled for them both to remain patient ordering that the great doors should be closed. Queen Guinevere, elegant as ever, kept her composure. Gawain eyed the Knight for any sign or signal of who he might be and Merlin, too, did the same. "King Arthur of the impotent land, I might say," the Knight smirked, "I have come to challenge you or any of your warriors brave enough to take up the challenge. Not that you will, cowards that you are."

He spoke his insults with an arrogance which was too much for Gawain. "I'll take it up," retaliated the impetuous young warrior. "You don't come here to insult the King in order to return without a fight. Before all here, I take up your challenge, I will kill you before we eat dried fruit."

The Green Knight condescendingly ignored Gawain before speaking once more to the King. "King Arthur, my challenge is simple but true. One of you, who it is I do not care, may take a single blow here and now at me with my axe but in return in one year and a day, he must receive a single blow from me." The King was quick to reply. "Sir Knight," he said, "I am happy with this bargain and will myself take up the challenge."

"My King," interjected Lancelot, "not so, not so. We don't know who this apparition is or what evil power he has. One of us must accept the challenge in your place, we cannot risk you."

"I agree with Lancelot," added Sir Owain and there was a silence as both Lancelot and Owain looked towards Arthur's Counsellor. "Merlin, do you agree?" Lancelot asked. Merlin diplomatically replied, "Gawain has already stated his determination to undertake this challenge. He did so before us all and before the King spoke and if he is still of the same mind, then I believe he should be the one to respond to the Green Knight."

"I want him," cried out Gawain clambering over a table, "I'll have his head off with one blow and bathe in his green blood for good measure."

"If that be so, then the challenge is yours," the King confirmed.

The Green Knight indolently ran his finger along the blade of a green axe which lay at his side and brazenly asked, "Is your debate concluded? Am I to kill this young man called Gawain, this impetuous Knight who speaks before he thinks?"

"You are to face Sir Gawain, a man worth more than a hundred apparitions such as you," retorted the King, adding, "Gawain has the challenge."

"Then Sir Gawain, come to me and receive my axe. With it you may give me one blow and in return in twelve months and one day, you will meet with me when I will return your blow with one of my own."

"And where will that be?" asked Gawain as he prepared himself to slice off the Green Knight's head.

"At the Green Chapel," replied the Knight coolly. Gawain made no response to this but rather took the hefty green axe from the Knight. The Green Knight dismounted from his horse and asked, "Would you like me to stand or to kneel?"

"Stand where you are," replied Gawain. And so the Green Knight stood before Gawain bearing his green flesh about his neck for Gawain and all to see. Gawain held the axe firmly in both hands. "Now foul man," he said, "prepare for your end."

"No need to get excited," replied the Green Knight calmly. "I am prepared and always have been."

With one sweeping movement, Gawain then cut through the neck of the standing Knight so that the head fell immediately to the floor. The momentum of Gawain's stroke took the axe in one huge arc so that Gawain was bent over as the head dropped in front of him. Gawain watched it roll beneath the tables where the warriors kicked at it. There was at first a roar of laughter and applause, but it was quickly followed by an eerie silence. The eyes in the head under the table stared at Gawain and one seemed to wink at him as the head was being buffeted from one warrior to another. The silence, however, halted the insult of the game as all began to realise that the body of the Green Knight remained erect, standing on his own two feet. Headless and upright it remained, a terrible sight, as its green blood spurted upwards in a grim fountain of defiance. Kay jumped over the table and ran up to the body and pushed it but it would not fall down. Everyone froze as the blood ceased to flow. Slowly the body walked towards its severed head and bending down, with its right hand picked up the head by its green hair. Gawain was still crouched down on the floor, but rose eye to eye with the ghastly sign as the green head spoke.

"Sir Gawain, Sir Gawain," it said solemnly, "you have given me a stroke which was strong and true. Be you as strong and true in yourself. I will meet you at the Green Chapel in one year and a day. Until then I wish you and all this company well." Then the body with its left hand took the green axe from Gawain, before with its head in one hand and the axe in the other, it leapt onto its horse which turned and trotted towards the great doors which the King ordered to be opened. Gafallt was guarding this exit as he had done since the Green Knight had entered. The dog tensed itself and bared its teeth as if it were going to take the head from the Green Knight's hand. Then the Green Knight's eyes flashed for a moment as the Knight's right hand turned the green head to face the King, whilst the left hand threateningly raised the axe.

"Gafallt," King Arthur commanded, "let him pass." The dog growled and approached his master in a small triumph of his own. "Good dog," the King said as the Green Knight left the hall on his green horse, the hooves of which hit the stones outside so hard that sparks flew from them before in an instant the horse and headless rider were gone. The doors were shut, locked, barred and bolted. No one spoke. Gawain looked pensive for a while before walking solemnly to his King. He knelt saying, "Sir, I beg that when the time comes, I may leave your company to fulfil the challenge which has been witnessed by all."

"Sir Gawain," replied the King with equal solemnity, "you have my blessing and my good will and at the appointed time, you may leave for your quest with our faith and our love."

A cheer went up and the courtiers banged on the tables and shouted out Gawain's name. Merlin signalled to the servants who quickly cleansed the room of the green blood whilst King Arthur talked in private to Gawain. After a while the King resumed his place, turned to his warriors and silenced them all. He bent down and again patted his brave dog before rising and saying with a wry smile, "My warriors and ladies all here present," he paused, "now thanks to Sir Gawain, I shall eat." With that he beamed at Merlin, shook the hand of Gawain and of Lancelot and kissed his Queen. Owain returned the King's cloak to him and robed him in it. King Arthur looked supreme, the burning fire reflecting in his golden hair. Guinevere was happy and as beautiful as the poets said whilst Lancelot was gracious and content. Gawain having resumed his seat continued to receive the adulation of everyone with the feasting lasting well into the night. The land was to find stability again resulting in good order since a new quest had begun.

Was it a long year or a short year for Gawain? It is hard to say. Excitement may have shortened it, anxiety lengthened but what of fear? He must surely have been frightened having sliced off the green man's head only to find that the body did not fall and that defenceless, therefore, he was duty bound to receive a similar blow himself at a place he had to find without even a clue being given as to where it might be. The Green Knight had only instructed Gawain to meet him in a year and a day at the Green Chapel. The Chapel, the warriors concluded was not within their own realm, yet they knew that the Green Knight had clearly been watching their conduct throughout the whole of the previous year and probably the present one, so they deduced the Chapel could not be far from their own boundaries. They knew it could not be to the South from where they recently had returned, or to the East which they had fortified or to the West, since they knew every ridge, vale and valley of that land to the sea. They surmised that it had to be, therefore, to the inhospitable North where the great mountains lay with their lakes and marsh lands. That was a green and grey coloured land, a damp bog land green, infused by the grey of death. Merlin advised Gawain to ride North, over the great river towards the forbidding mountains where he and the King believed Gawain would find the Green Chapel and the Green Knight's domain.

So it was that in autumn, Gawain appeared before the King and asked permission to leave so as to take up his quest against the apparition that had challenged the whole court and its civilisation. The Green Knight had cheated death, could Gawain now do the same? There was admiration for him, but there was also apprehension, even fear as formally he approached the King and said, "Sir, I come to ask leave to fulfil the quest of the New Year. I wish to journey to the Green Chapel and honour my promise to the Green Knight."

The King replied, "Gawain, you have my permission to leave and my hopes go with you." Until now it had been as if Gawain's adventure was nothing but a dream but seeing him a brave, lonely figure kneeling before the King, brought many people to the verge of tears. The King too was sad since within Gawain he saw himself and recalled his own youthful fears. Despite all the stories about these courageous warriors, they were only men, having the same doubts and concerns as all men when faced with difficult challenges to the point of death. For Gawain there seemed little hope, the risk was immense. Unarmed and exposed he had to receive a single blow, from a devil of a man, an apparition that brought fear into the hearts of all who saw him. It appeared to be a lost cause and the company feared they would never see their brave friend again, with his eager interruptions, his joy of life and his love of the King and all who followed him.

Gawain's leaving for the quest was an unforgettable sight. His sword, helmet and shield had been laid out on a red carpet. He was dressed in the finest cloth over which came a tunic made of silk, lined with the softest fur. Over this was a metal breastplate, tied around the back with thick leather straps. It was overlaid by a cape woven by the good people of Bardsey Island and given to the King for his protection but he had ordered that it was to be given to this brave warrior.

Gawain privately spoke with the King for some time. Merlin didn't fully know what was said and could only speculate that in each of the King's warriors are all of his warriors and in all of them, the King himself. Gawain was to be resolute, he should keep true to his word and consequently true to himself, or words to that effect. So it was that once Gawain was ready, his horse, Gringolet was brought to him by Tag, his servant boy. The horse was perfectly groomed and had been given a gold harness. As Gawain courageously mounted it, a Knight, who dressed always in black, presented him with a helmet which was covered with jewels. "Wear it well," he said.

Lancelot next approached with Gawain's sword and Owain brought him his shield, emblazoned with a pentangle after which it was called, a five pointed star ending where it begins. The shield had been designed specifically for him at King Arthur's command by the Master Blacksmith of the Fort to represent the five senses of man. Everyone felt so proud to see such a great warrior venturing out on an unknown and dangerous journey.

So as Gawain departed, as brave a man as anyone could imagine, a cheer was heard above the horn blast as he passed through the fortress gate and along the beaten track towards the wilderness. At the first bend he found Merlin waiting for him and looked down from his horse into the Counsellor's face where he saw sadness in the wise man's eyes. "I can help no more, my Gawain," Merlin said. "Take care. Remember that the King lives in you." Pausing and holding back the tears he continued, "And know this, I regard you and love you more than any man in the world except for the King."

Gawain placed his hand on Merlin's shoulder looking into his eyes and then touched his cheek, "You are the greatest friend a man could ever have." He gently nudged his horse to leave. Merlin watched him as he rode on and from the fortress ramparts, King Arthur and Queen Guinevere also watched till he disappeared from view. In a dark corner at the back of the stables, Tag, his young servant curled up in the straw and cried.

After days of riding, the weight of the breastplate beneath his cape began to pull him down, tiring both him and his horse. He knew that those who had given it to him meant well, but he unstrapped it at a place named Tabor, a settlement in the hills below Cadair Idris. It was a symbolic moment for him as it seemed to confirm the isolation of the quest which he was to undertake. He therefore buried it near a copse of trees below the mountain and there called on Idris that all would be well.

As he travelled Northwards, his trials began. Attacked on every side by beasts and flying insects as large as birds, Gawain ducked and weaved his way along paths which sometimes only took him back to a place where he had been before so forcing him to start and think again. His faithful horse became weak and tired yet still Gawain fought beast and animal, insects and huge spiders larger than his boots. He was forced to feed on the foul creatures he killed and so kept himself alive. Wearily leading his horse, he trudged off the paths and into the marshes. As the weeks passed, he gradually edged Northwards searching with his exhausted eyes but could see nothing resembling a chapel of any kind of colour.

On he trekked to where he approached a wide river which he and Gringolet waded across and then a narrower one no more than a rivulet, before arriving at a barren plain from where he continued to ride further North into the bleak mountains beyond peppered with cold lakes. There seemed no end to the torment of his ride until on the Eve of the Midwinter Festival he glimpsed a fortress on a high plateau that levelled out just below a mountainous ridge. "Green Chapel or not," he thought, "this is where I will rest. Perhaps I will receive good food and the people will care for Gringolet." But the deeper thought that crossed his mind was that perhaps this was the place where his adventure would come to its end. The fort was a magnificent sight dominating the plain with the sheer cliff face of the ridge behind it just like Arthur's camp in the South. The closer he got, however, the more impressive it became. He had never seen anything quite like it for in addition to a single impressive hall rising above the outer fence, the fortress had four square imposing towers built of stone each positioned at the perimeter wall which likewise was made from large stones. The great hall, built in the very centre of the encampment, towered higher than any he had seen in Arthur's kingdom. All was painted in bright colours which deliberately drew attention to itself as an impenetrable, magical fortress. High above flew a standard which depicted a ferocious, green boar on a yellow background. Climbing higher to the entrance of the fort, Gawain found that it was protected by a moat on all sides forcing him to shout a greeting across the water.

"Who calls?" a voice sounded.

"I am a warrior of King Arthur who seeks food and shelter this season," he yelled in reply. "My name is Gawain, and I come in peace."

"Enter," came a warm response as a heavy wooden drawbridge was lowered, "and find what you will."

Was it that he had arrived at his journey's end? Although this place didn't appear anything like a chapel, it was beyond the realms of anything he had experienced on earth. It was a mysterious, mystical otherworldly vision of a fortress, as intimidating in its overwhelming size as the Green Knight had been in his grotesqueness seated on his green horse. Gawain looked up at the standard where the colour of the boar did not escape his notice. Perhaps at least, he thought, this seat of power built high on the mountain side would provide some answers to the riddle of the Green Knight and his whereabouts. He put these thoughts to the back of his mind since he wished only for food, company and a rest over the festive days before taking his leave to continue his quest. If the Green Chapel was not here it had to be found whatever the welcome he was to be given. It was quite simply a matter of truth: of being true to himself and to the word he'd given to the apparition and to his King.

So it was that he entered the fortress in view of the inquisitive people for whom it was their home. Little did he know that in one of the towers locked away but seeing everything, King Arthur's enemy, Morgen was watching out for him. Her time would soon come as she had once prophesied to destroy the King by driving a wedge between his warriors. Mordred, exploiting a foolish decision by Agravain to announce the Queen's relationship with Lancelot, was to be the means to cause the civil war which would ensue. But for now, she was imprisoned in a room where she had been confined by the master of the fortress where Gawain had arrived. It was here that she was locked with her evil thoughts, the hell of her being. Although she was rarely allowed out of her room, she could see all below. She could plot and send messages to her supporters and she knew what she would do if anyone failed on a quest. Had Lancelot already behaved shamefully with Guinevere? Had Gawain lost his strength on his journey in defeating the beasts and insects that she had sent to destroy him? These were the questions that tormented her brain as she squinted to see if the stranger was, as she hoped and feared, Gawain.

The sun was setting as the servants and boys gathered round the visitor and his horse. Gringolet would be pampered over the Festive period and the animal seemed to sense what was in store as it trotted off eagerly with a young boy called Eldred, who one day would become a great King. He washed and brushed Gringolet down, bathing the sores and feeding him on the best hay that they had. Meanwhile the Chieftain of the fort, accompanied by his wife had come out to greet the stranger.

"Welcome," he said to Gawain, "what brings you here and why during this Midwinter season?"

Gawain replied with courtesy, "I am of King Arthur's realm on a quest begun almost a year ago. My name is Gawain and I'm looking for shelter."

"You are welcome to our shelter and our food," the Chieftain replied. "My name is Bercilak and I insist that you stay for the festivities to come. You have arrived at Caercilak and I hope you will accept the hospitality of one who admires your King. Rest and refresh yourself and we will meet over dinner when you can tell us of your quest and King Arthur's realm." Then raising his voice so all those who stood around could hear, Sir Bercilak said, "It is a great honour that we, this Festive time, should entertain a warrior-knight from King Arthur's realm. Arthur is a King whom we love and respect as will be shown in the kindness we extend to his Knight, Sir Gawain." Turning again to Gawain he said, "I long to hear of King Arthur and of his warriors and of Merlin. But we will have time for that and more so go in my friend, and rest."

With that, Gawain entered the vast hall, followed by his host and his wife who had welcomed the stranger with a courteous smile. As they approached the doorway, the Chieftain looked up to the turret from where Morgen was peering. He then turned to Gawain with a mixture of affection and concern on his face and placed a hand on his shoulder.

On the eve of the Midwinter festivity, the custom was kept to eat simple food in preparation for the celebrations the next day so that night the entertainment was modest but throughout it Gawain was encouraged to talk of his home and of his adventures in reaching Bercilak's lands. The young warrior, as he spoke, impressed Bercilak through his obvious loyalty to his King and Queen and love of his companions. The next day entertainments took place and stories of the Chieftain's sea voyages were told. Gawain heard of monsters emerging from the depths and of mighty waves which would have overwhelmed the ships but for the courage of Bercilak's followers. Gawain was then encouraged to tell the stories of King Arthur, which were so vivid that it was as if Arthur and his warriors were there with him.

In the evening, Bercilak escorted to dinner not only his young and beautiful wife, but also the old lady from the tower. Gawain was told that she was a recluse living for her own safety in the care of the Chieftain but her name was not revealed. She said nothing throughout the festive meal but ate, drank and watched. Then accompanied by the young hostess and other ladies, she left the room as the custom was for the men to sing songs and tell more stories of violent battles.

So the feast day came and went with good humour. Gawain checked the chapel as he attended the day's rites with Sir Bercilak, but he did not find even a hint of green. The following day, therefore, Gawain asked his host's permission to leave. "But why," Bercilak asked, "why leave us so soon?"

Gawain then told his tale of his search for the Green Chapel where he must meet with the Green Knight on New Year's Day. "Don't worry," Bercilak reassured him, "your quest will be completed since the Chapel which you describe is not far from our own fortress, a ride of no more than two hours. On the appointed day I will have a guide take you there."

Gawain was pleased, although he felt some fear as he heard the news. If he had not found the Chapel, honour would have been tainted but his life spared. He put that latter thought firmly from his mind, smiled and thanked the Chieftain agreeing to stay until the appointed time which greatly pleased his host. "Now," Bercilak said, "Gawain, I will have a bargain with you. Rest here and be in charge of my fort while tomorrow I go hunting. The prize I gain in my hunt I will give to you on my return and whatever you gain in this fortress you can give to me." Gawain agreed, and the bargain was confirmed with them shaking hands on a pact of brotherhood and trust, which Morgen observed with relish.

Bercilak rose the next morning before dawn and after a breakfast with his men left the fortress to go on the hunt. The horns blasted, the dogs were set free and the deer began to panic at the sound and ran towards the forest, but as Bercilak's beaters had waited behind them, they drove the deer back into the fields. There the Chieftain saw a stag which he decided was for him. The chase which began lasted all day. Deer were killed on the way but this magnificent stag was the one Bercilak wished to hunt down to give to Gawain, his guest.

Meanwhile Gawain slept through the dawn, waking at the noise of the horses leaving the yard. From the seclusion of his bed around which drapes were hung to keep out the cold, he heard the door of his lodging open slowly. He wasn't alarmed since he kept his dagger sheathed close to him. Cautiously he peered through the drapes and saw Bercilak's wife entering the room. She was as beautiful as Guinevere and as fresh as the morning itself. Her skin was pure white, smooth as shining marble. Her hair hung down over the bodice of her gown which was embroidered with gold lace but the top three clasps were open, allowing the tantalising hint of her beauty.

Gawain pretended to sleep closing his eyes fast shut and breathing deeply as if in a dream but the lady came quietly over to his bed and drawing back the drapes sat on it and waited. Gawain also waited feigning sleep for some time but the lady was in no hurry. Gawain at last decided that he would have to move as if waking so he turned slightly in the bed. She watched him with her pure emerald eyes as he stretched a little and then started as if by surprise on seeing her. "Madam," he said, "you startled me."

"To startle one of King Arthur's warriors is an achievement," she laughed.

"I expect it is, Madam," he replied.

"And to love such a man must be something which any woman might wish."

Gawain swallowed hard, surprised at her boldness and yet he could not offer her any offence. He thought quickly and said, "Madam, it might prove one of disappointment not fulfilment and therefore is a matter of no thought."

"That is not what I hear from the stories of Arthur's warriors."

"Madam," he answered, "you must not believe all you hear in stories."

She laughed but the awkward moment for Gawain had passed. She then questioned him about the ladies in King Arthur's realm, what they wore and how they lived their lives. She was most interested in Guinevere as she had heard that she was so very beautiful. Gawain answered all her questions as well as he could and after an hour or so of talking, she kissed him on the cheek and left.

Out on the hunt Bercilak had the royal stag trapped on a plain that led to the sheer cliffs of the mountain. The beast ran hard and the Chieftain and his huntsmen had to keep up. The dogs were disciplined as the hunt was not theirs but that of their master. He wished no pain for this magnificent animal so he shot one arrow which pierced the heart and the great stag fell. Quickly the huntsmen made sure their quarry was still then they skinned it and prepared it, returning in triumph to the fortress as evening set it. Gawain was waiting for them and greeted them in front of the roaring fire. Bercilak called for his prize and presented the deer to his guest.

"Our bargain, Gawain," he beamed, "was for me to present you with the prize of the day."

"It was, Sir," replied Gawain, "and I in return am to give you what I gained here."

With that Gawain clasped his host in his arms and kissed him on the cheek before the company. "A worthy gain, Sir

Gawain, but I ask no questions in accepting the gift." He laughed and all about laughed with him, including Gawain. "Tomorrow," the Chieftain continued, "we will renew our bargain. My prize in the field will be yours and what you gain will be mine." The two men embraced as Gawain agreed, "It's a bargain," and they went in for dinner.

Early the next day before the sun had risen Bercilak was up ready for the hunt. He again ate breakfast before leaving with his huntsmen and dogs to hunt one of the wildest of animals, the ferocious boar. For this hunt Bercilak wore a cap in the shape of his intended victim. The horses were nimble and fast whilst the hounds were hungry, keen and ready for the kill. Gawain asleep in his bed didn't even hear the clamour of the horses in the courtyard below but soon after daybreak he was woken by a noise at his door. He again looked from behind the drapes and saw Bercilak's wife.

"Good morning, Gawain," she greeted him, "and what pleasure would you wish from me on this wonderful day?" she asked climbing onto the bed next to him.

"Good morning, Madam," he replied, "the spring has not come and all is dormant until the warmth of April."

She laughed and said, "But in warmth might there not be silent growth?"

"Silence," he answered, "is for monks who daily constrain their bodily growth."

She laughed again, "Tell me, Gawain," she implored, "more stories of Arthur and his friends. What entertainments are there other than those of men in arms?"

So the moment of temptation having passed, Gawain talked to her about the banquets and the feasts and the humorous debates about love and faithfulness which always ended in a vote by the warriors and the ladies of the court. "And who wins the vote?" she questioned him. "Madam, the vote is always won by the ladies," he answered. "And so it should," she responded and with that gave him two kisses, one on each cheek and left the room.

Gawain breathed a sigh of relief since despite his weakness, he had endured temptation. The lady was so beautiful that he longed to love her but as a true warrior he would betray his honour since she was his host's wife. Gawain felt pleased that he had not fallen into such a disgrace.

Meanwhile the hounds had found the boar or rather the boar had found the hounds. Some returned bleeding to their masters whilst others lay strewn on the field, never to hunt again. Bercilak and his huntsmen followed the track into the woods, out onto scrubland and then back into the dark woods. The remaining hounds kept their distance from the boar but still went onwards with their masters. Suddenly a cry was heard from one of the huntsmen who had the boar cornered by a waterfall. The rest of the huntsmen joined him immediately but Bercilak being further away was slower in getting to them. His men shot their arrows but they couldn't penetrate the boar's thick hide. One of the men rode too close to the animal and his horse was gored by the boar's enormous tusks, the huntsman only narrowly escaping with his life, ran back to the others for safety. Although the trapped boar could not escape, the men could not defeat it. This was the picture when the Chieftain arrived: the boar was backed towards the waterfall, the dead horse lay in the stream, to the sides were the huntsmen with their backs to the trees their dogs barking and snarling. The boar's head was twisting and turning and foaming at its mouth. Bercilak took in the scene and dismounted from his horse.

"Sir, be careful," cried one of his men.

"Don't be frightened and don't distract me," Bercilak commanded.

He strode into the stream, skirting around the dead horse. The boar snarled and Bercilak froze in concentration. There was only one vulnerable place at which he could strike as no dart, no sword would pierce the skin except between the eyes. The Chieftain lifted his sword above his head, grasping its hilt in his two hands. This exposed his body to the sight of the wild animal. Bestial brain was set against human bravery as the boar charged through the water, hurling itself at the warrior. Bercilak seemed to remain frozen but as the sharp pointed tusks came near to his heart, he dived to the right, thrusting his sword between the beast's eyes. A chilling yell was heard across the wood. Bercilak fell into the stream, the boar shedding its blood, falling across his chest. The huntsmen came to their master's aid but as they heaved the animal from him he cried out jubilantly, "Don't worry, my ribs are strong and the day is ours."

"And your aim was perfect," exclaimed one of the huntsmen pointing to the sword still locked in the brain of the dead animal. All cheered their Chieftain as Bercilak removed his sword from the beast's head. The carcass was cleaned, the offal given to the dogs and the boar tied to a pole by its legs and carried back to the fortress.

Horns signalled their return as Gawain waited in the hall by the fire. Bercilak had his men bring in the trophy of the day and presented it to his guest. "Sir, what a ferocious animal that was," Gawain cried out in admiration, "but now it must be cooked for our evening feast." As the boar was taken to the kitchens, Gawain in front of the whole company grasped Bercilak in his arms, and as much as it was honourable to do so, he gave the host two kisses, one on either cheek.

"Ah," laughed Bercilak, "so you have triumphed once more. But I ask no questions in giving my prize and accepting yours." Gawain replied, "Sir, I have kept my bargain but soon it will be New Year's Eve and I ask that I might leave to resume my quest." The host replied jovially, "Do not worry, I told you the place you need to find is not far from here. On New Year's Day a guide will show you the spot and your quest will be completed." Gawain agreed, "Sir, I trust you and will wait as you say." "A good answer, Sir Gawain, so let us have one final bargain. On New Year's Eve the prize of my hunt will be yours but whatever you gain here will be mine." Gawain was pleased to accept. "A deal it is then," Bercilak confirmed, "tonight and tomorrow we will feast on your boar." Gawain laughed, "On the boar, Sir, which you bravely killed." "And so I did," the host proudly admitted and then the tale was told by the huntsmen of the charge of the boar, the slaying of the horse and the bravery of their Chieftain.

The feasting continued well into the night and the next day but on New Year's Eve before dawn Bercilak rose and ate breakfast. He went out to the courtyard and led his huntsmen and his dogs on a third day of adventure. This time the fox being their intended prey, the dogs set off to find the scent. High up in her tower, Morgen heard them leave and smiled to herself as she imagined the end of King Arthur's kingdom and the breaking of his stronghold.

Gawain slept through the din, the clatter of the horses, the barking of the dogs, the sounding of the horns but he awoke suddenly on hearing the door of his room open. Bercilak's wife entered the room and appeared more beautiful than ever. She moved swiftly to the bed and got in beside Gawain placing herself close to his body and laying her hand on his cheek. "My Lady," he said, "you are as beautiful as the Mayday sun, but as vulnerable as a spring flower. I love you but I am not your husband although all that I am longs for you. I will not offend you by my selfish desires. I remain faithful to you and Sir Bercilak." "Oh Gawain," she replied, "you are an honourable man. I wish I had met you before my husband." "Not so, My Lady, your husband is brave and good." "And so he is," she agreed. Then covering herself and sitting on then bed she questioned Gawain some more about his quest. He told her of the Green Knight and of the challenge. All this she knew but he went further and he told her of his anxiety, confessing his fear that this might be his last day on earth.

"Not so, not so, not so," she insisted kissing him three times, once on each cheek and once on his forehead. She then rose from the bed and turning to him said, "Gawain, I have offered you my heart, my body, myself, but you have refused all three and so I ask you now to receive one gift from me which must remain a secret between the two of us. I have a scarf as a girdle round my waist which I ask you to wear. It was made by magic and will protect the wearer from violence of any sort. Wearing it you cannot die. Take it from me and wear it tomorrow as you meet the gruesome knight."

With that she removed the green scarf from her waist and gave it to Gawain. Politeness dictated that he had to accept this gift; protection determined that he must wear it on the following day and honour ensured that the gift would remain a secret. He took the gift from her with thanks and she left his room. He sat on the bed looking at the green cloth, contemplating the possibility of his death the next day. His only hope was the magic of this scarf which he hid in his room, determining that he would wear it to face his adversary.

Morgen slept soundly in her bed. Out in the fields the scent of the fox had been found. The animal, hunter of hens and chickens bringing disaster to households dependent on its victims, cunningly wound its way through brambles and bracken. The hounds were pricked and scratched in their chase, then, it went into water, out again and back into the stream where it made its way upward towards its lair. The dogs at first were confused but soon the leader of the pack picked up the scent again. The horns sounded and Bercilak led the chase. The cunning fox was seen and Bercilak instructed his men to shoot. A single volley of arrows killed the fox whilst the hounds were held back—there would be no aimless butchery. The fox was skinned, its entrails fed to the pack and so the hunt returned home to Caercilak.

Gawain standing in front of the fire, welcomed his host. "Sir," he said, "before you present me with your prize, here is mine." With that Gawain took Bercilak in his arms and in front of the whole company kissed the Chieftain three times, once on each cheek and once on his forehead. "Sir Gawain," laughed Sir Bercilak, "you do me honour by the love that was given to you. I ask no questions as the bargain is fulfilled and here receive my prize."

With that Gawain was given the skin and head of the fox. There was great joy and merriment which lasted into the night's feast. As it concluded, Bercilak spoke solemnly, "Tomorrow, Gawain you must be up early. First thing in the morning my guide will take you to the Green Chapel which I warn you, is a dangerous place. We would like you to stay here with us but we know that for you, because of your honour and truth it is not possible. You are a brave man and we will let you go." "Sir," replied Gawain, "I am prepared." "I will see you before you leave," said Bercilak as Gawain went to his bed.

From her high tower, Morgen looked at the stars and breathed deeply. All would be as she wanted but as she stared she saw one star shining brighter than the rest which seemed to cluster all others about it. A cloud hid it from view for a while and then another but each time the clouds dispersed, the star and the companions would appear again brighter than before. "That star," she said to herself, "will never dim whatever the clouds do, whatever I wish. Cursed be that star," she cried, "my curse upon it." With that she closed the casement window and pretended that the sky was nothing but an empty void, black and soulless. But this was a star that could never be destroyed since it was her sister Seren looking down on the world and all its activities.

Oh that Morgen might have remained for ever in her dark pain and her evil thoughts and that they might have devoured her heart, since she had no goodness to redeem her, her whole self being evil. No one could bring love to her, no not Gawain, nor Lancelot, not Merlin, not even King Arthur himself nor his forbear Idris, her father whom she hated with an intensity that defied understanding to the point that there was nothing in her but hate itself.

By dawn the next morning Gawain was in the courtyard. A squire had dressed him in clothes that looked as fresh as the day he had said farewell to King Arthur. A girl brought Gringolet to him, rested and bright from the attention given to him over the festivities. Morgen's casement window remained shut. Sir Bercilak and his wife on hearing that Sir Gawain was ready to depart came down for the farewells.

"Gawain," the Chieftain said, "it makes my wife and me sad that you should leave us today but your word is your oath and that can't be broken. Words should not be set against words, they should complement each other. The truth is what matters and you have been true to the words you spoke and those words will always remain."

"Sir," replied Gawain, "you speak wisely. I must go and whatever happens, know that next to King Arthur, I hold you in the highest esteem as I respect and honour your wife next to my Queen, Guinevere, as the most radiant, courteous and admirable Lady in the world."

"Go on your way," Bercilak commanded warmly, "and return the winner of your quest."

Gawain's eyes fleetingly fell to the ground but he quickly fought his anxiety. "Sir," he continued, "if I am to die, I will die. If I am to return, I will return."

"So be it, Gawain. Now ride from the fort towards the crossroads where you will be met by my guide who will then take you the way you want to go."

"Thank you, Sir, and farewell."

"Farewell, Sir Gawain," said the Chieftain. For a moment as they looked into each other's eyes, there was a depth of sadness in both which smiles, confidence and good wishes could not disguise. The wind blew across the courtyard and the cold casement blinds rattled in the winter sun. Sir Bercilak's lady stepped forward, "Go bravely, Sir Gawain, and come back safely to us both." She looked into his eyes but he turned his from her. Under his tunic he wore her scarf but he would not betray her though he might betray himself. Was he to trust himself or to trust in the magic he had been given?

"Farewell," he said smiling at his hosts, "thank you."

Gringolet turned and Gawain rode from the fortress on what might prove to be his final adventure. At the crossroads, just as Bercilak had said, he was met by a young guide. "Sir Gawain," he enquired formally, "which way do you want to go? The way you came is the fortress, the way to your left is King Arthur's realm, the way in front leads to the sea and the way to the right is the Green Chapel."

"I will go to the right," Gawain unhesitatingly said.

"Follow me," said the guide and Gawain followed.

Soon the broad way petered out into a track, then into a rocky path and then into a field. When they reached the centre of the field, the guide stopped. "Gawain," he said, "I can't go any further. Over the hill at the end of this field, you will find a valley. Ride down into the valley and there you will find the Green Chapel. It is guarded by a violent deadly demon. No one who has entered the valley has ever returned. It is a terrifying place. I saw that demon once from the hill's ridge and never want to see him again. Gawain," the young man pleaded with the warrior, "turn back, go home. Don't go on."

"My friend," Gawain replied, "how I wish I could follow your advice but you know as well as I that I have a journey to complete and cannot go back." "I don't know you, Sir Gawain, but I do know that the valley is a terrible place and you should not wish to go anywhere near it."

Gawain laughed, "That is impossible, leave me now and thank you for your help."

With that the guide turned and rode away. Gawain watched him until he disappeared along the path that they had come. In his head Gawain could hear only the voice of the Green Knight, "Be you as strong and true in yourself. I will meet you at the Green Chapel in one year and a day."

Gawain looked to the pentangle on his shield as he spurred his horse towards the hill which was steeper than it appeared and therefore proved a hard, steady climb. At the top he saw below him a deep green valley. Gringolet had become restless starting to neigh and rear. "Come my brave horse," Gawain encouraged the animal and down they rode defiantly into the valley. There they wandered looking for the Green Chapel but for a long time could find nothing. At the end of the valley there was a burial place, a barrow mound covered in green. He rode to it and saw that it was hollowed out. A man could enter there and pray as a hermit might. "Is this the Green Chapel?" he thought. "Is this the Green Chapel?" he asked muttering the words to himself. "Is this the Green Chapel?" he yelled out with anger and annoyance at the top of his voice so that the winter birds flew from their nests in a cacophony of sound. There were so many birds that the sun was dimmed as they flew on their way. "If this is the Green Chapel," he shouted out, "here I stand, Gawain, of King Arthur's realm ready to discharge my debt to the one who challenged me one year and a day ago as I vowed I would."

Gawain listened for a reply but there was absolute silence. He waited in the quietness and eventually detected a faint sound coming from the other side of the crag behind the Chapel. He puzzled to identify the noise he could hear in this now peaceful place. He listened hard and realised it was that of a grinding stone, the burning of metal being sharpened. "Where are you?" he called out.

"Why Gawain, I am here," came the reply.

Gawain looked to the top of the crag where silhouetted against the dying sun, the Green Knight stood, tall and forbidding with the axe in his hand. "So, Sir Gawain," said the apparition descending in one leap from the crag, "you have come at your appointed hour, my compliments to you and to your King." "No need for compliments," replied Gawain, "I am here as I agreed to receive the blow you promised last New Year's Eve." The Green Knight approached him, "Then Sir Gawain, my axe is newly sharpened. Prepare your neck since you will pay the price of our bargain." "I am ready," answered Gawain as he knelt head bowed in front of the Knight, exposing the flesh of his neck for the blow.

There wasn't a sound to be heard. All the birds had flown, the wind had dropped and the earth didn't even creak or groan. Gawain kneeling there in the valley of the Green Chapel could only feel the beating of his heart in his knowledge of what was to be. The Green Knight raised his axe high and cried out, "Sir Gawain, receive the blow owed to you." But as the axe descended Gawain feeling the air rush close to his flesh, flinched. At once the Green Knight stopped the thrust of the axe.

"Gawain," he said angrily, "Gawain, did I flinch when in front of the court of King Arthur you sliced through my neck and let my head fall to the floor, where Arthur's unruly men kicked it? I didn't nor do I expect you here at my Chapel to flinch for one moment."

"Sir Knight," Gawain apologised, "I felt the air on my neck and flinched I admit. Raise your axe again and I will hold steady."

The Green Knight breathed deeply and raised his axe high. Gawain's head was bowed, his neck uncovered, his spirit as low as it could be. The axe descended and as it did so Gawain closed his eyes in terror. Immediately the Green Knight halted the weapon's downward motion.

"Sir Gawain," he asked, "is your spirit so low that you have no courage in the face of death? Why are your eyes closed? Was my spirit low when last New Year's Eve I rode into the hall of your King? Did I not smile? Didn't my eyes sparkle even as my head was severed by the blow from this very axe?"

"My Lord," said the desperate Gawain, "indeed all that you say is true. My spirit was low and my eyes closed but you teach me to be courageous even in the face of death and so I beg you give me your blow. I will not flinch. I will not close my eyes. My spirit will remain strong."

"Then again, Sir Gawain, prepare yourself for the blow," commanded the Green Knight.

Once more Gawain bowed his head exposing the flesh of his neck for the blow from the gruesome Knight, coloured so green that he was indistinguishable from the Chapel in front of which he stood. Gawain calmed himself. The axe was raised and hurtled down through the air. Sir Gawain felt the air on his neck but did not flinch. He thought of the pentangle, of his King and of the mighty Idris. His eyes remained open as within himself he felt a peace and strength unknown to him before. As the axe reached the exposed neck, the Green Knight shifted his aim so that it merely glanced at the flesh, drawing blood which fell onto the grass. At once Gawain jumped up and drew his sword shouting out, "Knight, the blow has been returned, now face me and let us fight until one of us is dead."

Gawain turned from left to right and all around him but the Green Knight had disappeared. He waited looking all around him and into the mouth of the Chapel, but he was alone. He felt the green scarf tight around his waist and quietly to himself thanked the lady for her gift. He was alive and the Knight was gone. He looked up towards the way he had come, where he saw someone looking for him, calling to him.

"Who are you?" Gawain called.

"Why do you not recognise me, my friend?" said the approaching figure.

Gawain peered at him still wondering, still cautious, his sword ready for action. The man who approached was holding a green axe, but he was no longer coloured green. Gawain slowly recognised him and then realised the significance of all that had occurred since his arrival in this barren land. He lowered his sword and sank to his knees and despondently cried out, "Sir Bercilak!" He felt deeply ashamed as Bercilak, the green axe still in his hand, came closer to him, laying the axe on the ground and gently placing his hands on the kneeling Gawain's shoulders.

"Gawain, my brave friend," he said helping him to his feet, "I tested you three times. The first stroke in the air was for the kiss my wife gave you and you returned to me. The second stroke of strength was for the two kisses my wife gave you and you returned to me. The third stroke which drew your blood but did not kill you was for the three kisses that my wife gave to you and you to me. The drawing of blood was for your dishonour in not giving me everything."

"Oh Sir Bercilak," cried Gawain, "here, take the green scarf which your wife gave to me. I kept it to protect my life but it has brought me everlasting shame. Strike Sir, strike me again."

"Not so, Sir Gawain, for who would not when tested, save his own life?"

"Sir," replied Gawain, "I set my word against my word. I failed."

The Chieftain placed his arms around the Knight and held him tightly as a father might do his son. "Gawain," he said, "no man is a god. We wish for perfection but none of us can achieve it since there is no perfection on this earth, where we stumble and fall. So come back with me to my fortress and rest before your journey home to your King and friends."

"Sir," replied the distraught Gawain, "I cannot. I must return with my shame."

"Not your shame," insisted the Knight, "but your fallibility as a man, the same fallibility found in us all, including your King and his closest friends. Soon even his warriors will disperse but he will know that the fame of all the deeds of his reign will last for ever."

With those words, Gawain and Bercilak took their leave of each other. Gawain mounted his horse and left the valley of the Green Chapel with a gash on his neck which would turn into a scar to remain with him for the rest of time. Sir Bercilak stood on the ridge of the hill and sadly watched the young warrior as he made his solitary way back to King Arthur's realm. He then descended into the valley and placed the axe in the chapel which he sealed, setting the green scarf over the doorway before returning home. A breeze blew in the valley of the Green Chapel and the green scarf was taken up into the air where it was caught by a great bird and taken away, and the quest, like this tale had come to an end.

SIX

MERLIN'S TREE

W as it possible that Merlin so famed for his wisdom, could find himself captured and imprisoned with little chance of escape? It was not only possible but became a reality.

A girl arrived at Arthur's camp and announced that she was the daughter of one of Arthur's Chieftains from an adjoining land whom the King had recently helped by sending Sir Peredur to his aid during an attack by witches. This Chieftain being disabled was known as the Lame One. Peredur was victorious in defeating the evil coven but also in falling in love with the Chieftain's daughter who now stood before them all. She was distraught at the return of Peredur to Arthur's fort and frightened for her father since the witches were regrouping for another assault.

The King verified the story with Peredur and immediately instructed him to take a small force to help the Lame One. Within hours the group set off and later, Merlin followed in order to give advice as might be needed. The Chieftain's camp was on a plain, backing onto a deep river bank, and on the opposite side of the plain stood the wood where the witches were gathering. When Peredur and his men arrived, he rode straight to the Lame One's fort where he was warmly welcomed but Merlin decided on his arrival, to do some spying. He disguised himself as a beggar and with a staff in hand, walked straight into the centre of the witches' coven. It was a brave move but perhaps also a foolish one for a person thought to be so wise. The witches on hearing that he was begging for food laughed and mocked that he was more likely to be made food for the crows than gain anything from them. He thanked them and went to depart but one of the witches tripped him up and as he stumbled, another pushed him so that he fell to the ground. He was now easy pickings as the witches surrounded him, howling and screeching, stamping on his hands, his legs and his back and kicking at his head. On and on they tormented him but he, saying nothing, endured the ordeal until quite suddenly, there was a silence and he realised that they had dispersed. From the ground with blood almost blinding his eyes, he saw three beautiful women walking towards him whom he perceived to be three of the daughters of Idris, Tanwen of the Fire, Morwen of the Sea and Seren of the Stars. No wonder the witches had retreated, he thought, as he tried to rise from the ground but passed out with the pain. When he awoke, his injuries had been tended, his wounds healed and his head, hands and feet anointed with an exotic cooling ointment, but he still felt weak. He looked for the sisters but they had gone, leaving him alone in the depths of the forest. He staggered to his feet and tried to walk and although stumbling he kept getting up, determined to find his way to the Lame One. But he was in the Wandering Wood whose paths refused him any escape to the plain beyond. Exhausted he fell again to the ground where with trepidation he heard the sound of approaching hooves and looking up saw a dark warrior riding towards him. It was the Black Knight, whom some say is the harbinger of life or death as time dictates. The dark warrior dismounted and lifted Merlin onto his horse leading him out of the forest where he gave him food and a drink which invigorated his whole body. No sooner had Merlin tasted the drink than, dreamlike, the Black Knight rode Northwards leaving the Counsellor on his own again.

Merlin believed that there was magic in the apparition and understood that the time had not come for him to die. He realised that there must be a task for him to perform of great importance whatever the subsequent cost. The three daughters of Idris had cured his wounds and anointed him with the most exquisite of balms and the Black Knight had given him food and drink of special properties as if to feed and sustain him for a long time. His learning told him that they were preparing him for a coming ordeal but he immediately put the thought out of his head as he had an errand given to him by Arthur which he was still to complete. Disguised still as the beggar, Merlin hobbled across the plain to the Lame One's fort which was closed to him until Sir Peredur's horse, sensing who the stranger was, neighed and stamped and Peredur understanding the signs gave orders that the beggar should be allowed to enter.

Merlin advised that there was no time to lose as the witches' force was amassing in huge numbers so a message had to be sent to Arthur asking for reinforcements. Peredur's horse was set free at the rear of the camp and galloped off to find the King who immediately on seeing it assembled a strong force himself and set out for the Lame One's lands hoping to arrive before the witches overwhelmed the fort.

But one further danger had been discovered by Merlin since even while he was being beaten, he had been surveying the coven and learned their leader's name. It was Morgen, the wayward daughter of Idris and she was expected imminently. The witches had to be distracted from their preparations for her arrival which would start the battle to come. So it was that Merlin ruled that he was the man to distract and delay them, refusing entreaties to the contrary. Insisting that he was the only one who could prevent the impending destruction of them all, he threw off his beggar's attire and in clothes fit for the Counsellor of King Arthur, ordered the gate to be opened. Proudly he walked out onto the plain taunting the hags, scoffing them and Morgen who was still expected. He cried out that he was Merlin and in him lay the authority of the King. Facing their massed forces he instructed them to be gone from these lands and return to the bogs and swamps, their natural home. Was this bravery or foolishness; wisdom or folly; confidence or conceit?

Imagine what then ensued, what delight the witches took in tormenting this trusted man and dear friend to the King. He was stripped and whipped just for their amusement and as night fell, they covered him in honey and left him tied to a tree so that when day broke the bees and wasps might engulf him and sting him to death. Perhaps that might have been a kinder fate than what occurred once Morgen arrived. Having instructed him to be washed, she interrogated him as to the secrets of Arthur's realm. Arrogantly he refused to answer her questions saying that he'd prefer to be hung from a tree and fed to the birds of the air than reveal anything to such as her.

She laughed and crowed that she could do better than that, boasting that her magic was greater than his. Merlin proudly derided her but she took no heed and had him tied to a tree which she then circled chanting a terrible curse which cast the dreadful spell on Merlin. Gradually in response to her chanting, the tree began to absorb the faithful Counsellor who slowly disappearing into it became entrapped within its wood and sap. With just Merlin's face visible, Morgen sadistically smirked and laughed at the torment she was inflicting on him, screeching, "Remain there for ever, for only a woman of life and death can free you and even I am not her. There is no and never will be such a woman." With that even Merlin's face was sucked into the bark and the inner fibres of the tree where the great Counsellor would be entombed for ever in his lonely, suffocating prison unless the curse could be removed.

Word came to the coven that Arthur had arrived with a mighty force and was preparing to fight at dawn. Morgen assembled her witches and the bloody confrontation ensued in which Arthur could have been defeated had he not remembered a Roman tactic in battle. The witches as well as fighting on the ground were flying above Arthur's warriors hurling fire on them, burning some to death. The King and his men retreated to the fort where he instructed every man to loosen his breastplate before they marched out again. Meanwhile, Morgen ordered all her troop to take to the air sensing that this was the most successful strategy against her enemy. It is what Arthur had predicted and as the fire started again to rain down on his warriors, he ordered them to raise their breastplates above their heads in one motion. The heat was so intense from the flames that it reflected back onto the flying hags and now scorched and burned many of them to death. The remainder retreated with Arthur's warriors pursuing them till most were killed but Morgen managed to flee with the remnants of her army.

The King who had learned the ways of the Wandering Wood and the secret of the ribbon of fire, went deep into its confines in search of Merlin, fearing that he might find him dead. Arthur at first could find no trace of him though Merlin from within his tree could see his King but had not yet found the magic to call out to him. Eventually Arthur found Merlin's clothes and then the remnants of the honey covered ropes discarded at the roots of the tree where Merlin was encased. The King rested against the tree in anguish, coming even eye to eye with his friend without being able to see him. Merlin desperately tried to shake the tree but he did not have the strength to call on his powers. Arthur feared that his friend had been tortured cruelly but as there was no sign of the body, he hoped and prayed that he had escaped. Sensing the stench from the stagnant lake nearby, Arthur as before, sadly called up the ribbon of fire to lead him from that place back to the plain beyond.

Only much later, when Morgen again battled with Arthur, did the King find out the dreadful truth of Merlin's fate and the curse that she had placed upon him until the woman of the prophecy might appear. But that is for another time.

SEVEN

LANCELOT AND GAWAIN

The revelation to the whole court was true; Guinever and Lancelot had committed adultery. An unfaithful Queen, a distraught King, a foolish friend were just people living their lives but all so human in their frailty. What price peace? What price loyalty? Sir Gawain was one of the first sacrifices to be made as Mordred, taking advantage of the situation, prompted the civil war with Lancelot that would bring Arthur's kingdom to an end. It was Gawain, however, who fought with Lancelot as both tried to avoid the slaughter of their companions. Young Tagit, known as Tag, who had witnessed his parents being killed at Pengwern, records the story in the following way.

Gawain appeared before the King and asked his blessing on the saddest quest that any of Arthur's Knights had ever undertaken, war against one of their own company, Lancelot. The desolate King, knowing well that the greatness of their fellowship was drawing to an end, grasped Gawain in his arms before the whole assembly saying, "My Gawain, be strong and wise and remember always this day, since I fear we may not meet again in these times." Gawain smiled at the King but I saw the tears in his eyes and I feared that what Arthur had said would prove sadly true.

Then, as now, in my mind's eye, I, Tag, watched the blessing and then, as now, in memory I heard the cheering of Gawain's army as we set off on the final journey. We marched from Arthur's Southern camp Eastward to our crossing over the River Severn. As we approached villages and settlements, people came to see us. Gawain was splendid in the armour which each night I kept spotless for him. His horse held its head high as proud as it should be. Gawain's shield, the same one as taken on the quest against the Green Knight, had on its front the pentangle and on the back, the picture of a beautiful woman of purity. But Gawain's sadness was evident for although he loved Arthur as his King, he loved beyond all thought his friend Lancelot and Guinevere, his Queen, whom he had served for so many years.

"Wretched betrayal," he muttered, "for a Knight of such renown as Lancelot to have done such a deed, to have broken his oath to the King, to have set love against loyalty, against vows. But as I go to fight him I can only think of the goodness within him and the glorious days of friendship between us all."

So, with a heavy heart, Gawain rode on. He had become as a father to me after the foul things that had happened to my parents. No one could have loved a master more than I did him except for Gawain in his love for Arthur and it was this love which spurred him on. What greater desolation could there be than to see the country torn apart through the curse of love? What greater agony for a good man such as Gawain to have to choose between two dear friends where his loyalty must lie? I knew the anguish in his heart and I knew that however hard he fought, Gawain was too kind and loyal a friend to kill Lancelot. I knew, as he rode, that he was going to his death.

Since the time of my rescue at Pengwern, I had been troubled by a deep thought which I hid secretly in my heart. I had not uttered it to anyone but now as we marched towards our port to sail to Brittany, I determined finally to talk out the whole matter with Gawain. We were camped not far from a settlement by the sea from where our army was to sail to Brittany. Gawain, though cheery with the warriors accompanying him, was sombre in private where I looked after him, but it was then that I decided to confide in him the darkness of my fear. I swallowed hard for I felt guilty even in the utterance of what I was to say. "My Lord," I began.

"Yes, Tag," he answered.

"My Lord, I have a worry in my soul which I need to tell you, if you would listen to me."

"Is it about Lancelot?" Gawain asked. "If it is, I would prefer you to keep it to yourself. Lancelot is a man I love almost as dearly as the King and far more than I love myself."

"My Lord, I do not want to speak about him but I do want to talk about love."

"Go ahead," Gawain replied.

"My Lord, why did my mother dance as she danced on that hateful day when my father was killed and she took her own life? Why did my father as Chieftain remain in that settlement believing the truce that had been made with the barbarian? Why didn't I, as young as I was, fall from the rafters onto the shoulders of the barbarian chief and cut his throat as he abused my mother? Why, my Lord, didn't I put a stop to all that I saw?"

Gawain got up from his seat and came over to me and put his arm around me. "Tag," he said, "you are to see such dreadful times and you, as young as you are, have already suffered much more than anyone ever should. But you ask

questions from your heart which shame me that I had not
anticipated them. What torments you have endured in the
memory of those days."

At this, Gawain put his hand to his neck where the scar
given to him by the stroke from the Green Knight remained.
He signalled me to sit with him and said, "Tag, your father
was wise and good and you were so young. You were the
future and he gave you a strict command—you were to
remain in those rafters. You were not to move until he or
a rescuer, came to your aid. If you had attempted to fight
the barbarian chief, you would have failed but more than
that you would have caused the death of your entire tribe.
You may have wounded the beast and who knows, in falling
from the rafters, knife in hand, you may have even killed
him, but you would have revealed your hiding place and
that of all the other children. The village would have been
set ablaze before King Arthur had time to arrive but you
obeyed your father and so saved the others. Your father was
a man of peace who detested conflict. He advised the King
that the way forward with the invaders was to make a truce
and allow them the lands in the East which we had lost. The
invaders had their pride and they had come for a new life
in a new land. We needed to show them and to persuade
them of the codes we practised and of the peace for which
we worked. Your father insisted that the King allow him his
settlement in that remote place believing that if an attack
were coming, he would sense its imminence and get word
to Arthur in time. The children would be taken to the forest to a secret encampment that had been built. The King
was watchful and feared that your father was mistaken and
that the attack would come without warning, which sadly it
did. For this reason the device of the false rafters was conceived which depended on your sister's speed of horse and

the King's supernatural powers. Your father laughed when the King told him he would fly as an eagle but attack as a bear and yet this is exactly what he did. His word was true but the barbarian's word was false. Your father had hoped that all words were as honest as his own. He was a just man and tried to do what was right.

"Now let me speak of your most difficult secret. The relationship between a man and a woman can be the greatest comfort but also the greatest weakness. Why else are we on this sad quest, for Lancelot has taken the Queen to himself? From your hiding place you saw things your father would not have wanted you to see. Your parents knew of the dangers and that day, your mother's only protection for you and the other children of the settlement was to use her beauty and her enchanting femininity. She danced as she could in the knowledge of the inevitability of her death and in doing so she looked in love to you, her innocence for ever more. Think not of her dance but of her look. The King has worked hard with his warriors to contain the barbarity that is within us all, to civilise it and you have witnessed the evil of which men are capable. In talking to me of your shame you have overcome the barbaric and triumphed, you are no longer my servant but my companion in arms." At that he held me tight in his love for me and I understood for the first time, the events of the past and felt contented although I feared what was to come.

We sailed from our port to a place in Brittany they called the Red Sunset. I remember as we arrived, the sun, warm on our backs, setting in the West as red as it could be imagined. Lancelot, our enemy, our friend, was there with Guinevere to greet us. None of us on either side wished to fight, and as companions that night the warriors from both sides shared a meal together. Once the meal was over, Lancelot invited

Gawain to his tent to talk. No one was allowed to join them, not even me, Tag, Gawain's loyal companion in arms.

The following day it was announced that there would be no fighting between the men loyal to Gawain and the King and Lancelot's supporters. No blood was to be shed on Breton soil but nevertheless, honour had to be defended and seen to be upheld. Gawain and Lancelot had agreed to meet in single combat on one of the ships that had carried Gawain across the sea. They would be attended only by their companions at arms and the fight would end in the death of one of them since no mercy would be shown by the victor. Their pact was that whoever died, his men would disperse in peace without being pursued, each man being allowed to choose a new lord to serve in future days. No one apart from the two companions at arms would see the fight and witness the death of a great warrior. This was their pact.

Before dawn the next day, Gawain and Lancelot rowed to the ship which lay in the harbour. I accompanied Gawain and Helleas accompanied Lancelot. As the sun rose over the land and dawn broke, Helleas and I agreed that the fight should start. With swords and daggers the two Knights fought throughout the morning and as the minutes and the hours passed, Gawain grew in strength, becoming more than a match for Lancelot, slicing through the leather fastening of Lancelot's breastplate which fell to the deck exposing the Knight's chest to Gawain's blade. Lancelot was all but defeated as the sun reached its height, when Gawain struck his opponent's sword so hard that Lancelot dropped his weapon from his hand and fell backwards onto the deck, with only his dagger to protect him. Gawain placed his foot on Lancelot's wrist so that the dagger was released and stood over his exposed breast with the sun directly above them. Gawain raised his sword and thrust it down, not into

Lancelot's heart but into the deck of the ship. He showed mercy to his friend. The sun moved and the afternoon came. Gawain pulled the sword from the deck and backed away from Lancelot. "I lost my aim," he lied.

"We made a vow," Lancelot said. "Your word was your word. You should not have set it against itself since it is the truth by which you live as once I did."

"And so it is still," Gawain replied as he threw Lancelot's sword back to him. "But I will not kill a defenceless man. This is the greater truth by which I live." He turned to Helleas, "Buckle him up," he ordered and turning to me said, "Give me drink." I gave him water and with sad determination he whispered, "It is the end."

They fought through the afternoon but just as Gawain's strength had increased with the rising to the midday sun, so it weakened from then to its sinking. As dusk approached and Gawain turned for breath, Lancelot found a weakness below his helmet. The Breton sword slashed through at Gawain's neck, twisting down into his breast and Gawain fell. Helleas called to his Lord to finish off the Knight's life. "There is no need," Lancelot replied pulling the weapon from the wound, "for he is as a dead man and will not survive." With that he signalled for Helleas to help him into a boat alongside and coldly left me with Sir Gawain. Another boat being rowed by two pages loyal to me carrying Manon my sister came up to our ship. Lancelot allowed the three of them to board and then set our ship free from its mooring and we drifted out to sea with the night tide.

I removed Gawain's armour. He was not dead as Lancelot knew but it was clear that death would eventually come. Gawain smiled at me and placed his hand to his neck. "It is on the other side," he said trying to laugh. "It is," I replied. "I'm glad," he answered, "for that scar from the

Green Knight has remained untouched and will go with me to my death and my life beyond it."

Manon tended to the wounded Knight whilst I took charge of the boat sailing it with the help of the two pages back to our lands. Life remained in Gawain and we landed at the port from where we had left. Did Lancelot, returning to his port, keep his word about sparing the lives of Gawain's men? I do not know, but I never saw any one of them again after leaving Red Sunset.

"There are five horses tethered in the woods," Gawain whispered as we neared our destination. We went to the forest and found the five horses and on his request we placed him on one. "No longer companion," he said to me, "but by the authority I have from King Arthur, I make you, Tagit the Young, known as Tag, a Knight for this day and forever more." He signalled for me to give him his sword and as I stood before him, Gawain almost slumping down on his horse, touched my shoulder with the blade, pricking my neck.

We journeyed Northwards since he wished to go to a place called Ogof y Meirw, the Cave of the Dead, where it was prophesied that King Arthur and his Knights would be buried. It was there he intended to rest awaiting their arrival. We reached Pengwern, where my parents had been killed, and riding onwards we could see the Welsh mountains to the North. Gawain was growing weaker by the day. Suddenly he sat himself up straight on his horse and looking across the valley to the land beyond he cried out his loyalty to his King. Then he relaxed, laying his head down on the creature's neck and holding on to its mane, he closed his eyes for the last time. We took him from his horse and laid him on the ground, resting his head on my sister's lap, with me kneeling beside them and the two pages kneeling at his feet. I felt at the temples of his head and then his wrists and said with tears in my eyes, my voice breaking, "Sir Gawain, the greatest of all our Knights, has gone and we remain alone." We wept for a while but strapping his body to his horse, we continued our journey. As we reached a valley reported to be not far from Ogof y Meirw, the Cave of the Dead, we were met by one of Arthur's warriors known as the Black Knight.

"It is almost over," he said continuing, "Tagit, the King commands that you leave Gawain and return to Pengwern where you are to make your home."

"But Gawain has made my brother one of King Arthur's Knights," my sister pleaded.

"That is a great honour," the dark warrior replied, "but the word of the King must be obeyed. Farewell."

With that he placed Gawain upright on his horse, supporting his back with poles and then rode gallantly towards the valley known as Cwm y Meirw and then around to the Heights of the Meirw beyond. My sister and I and her two companions, turned our horses round and retraced our steps back to the place of our childhood. With Gawain dead, we felt our world had gone. So it was and so it is that Tagit writes that you may know our sadness and our loss.

EIGHT
OGOF Y MEIRW

In earlier days on the return from his adventure at the Green Chapel Gawain had discovered the answer to one of the greatest secrets of King Arthur and his warriors: the final resting place where the King was to be taken after the civil war which would destroy his kingdom. In the story that follows, Sir Gawain, led by the gods or by mishap, arrived at Ogof y Meirw, the Cave of the Dead guarded by Corwen of the White Rock.

Re-entering King Arthur's lands after the adventure at the Green Chapel, Sir Gawain arrived at a fertile valley. He crossed the meandering river at its bottom and rode along its banks until he came to the far end of the valley where he was faced with a semi circle of rocks and cliffs allowing no exit. The only way out appeared to be to ride back. He smiled to himself as he recalled that a number of his companion warriors had complained that when journeying home from a quest, they'd entered a valley which had a dead end shaped in a huge arc of cliffs and slabs of rocks giving the impression of the markers of a massive grave or cairn. They named the place, therefore, Cwm y Meirw, the Valley of the Dead.

"Well," he laughed, patting his horse, "I suppose I've made the same mistake as many others I know. I'd better return the way I came and enjoy the peace and beauty of this valley as I ride." But as he made to turn he saw in the distance a woman near the cliff face. "Hello there," he shouted. The woman was bent over as if she were collecting something from the ground at the base of the cliff. "Hello there," he called again as he urged his horse to trot towards her. The woman slowly stood up and looked in his direction and at that Gringolet his horse immediately stopped. "What's the matter, Gringolet? Go to her. Go to her," he encouraged.

Gringolet remained still whilst the old woman looking at Gawain, raised her hand and motioned for him to join her. "Are you not well?" he called to her. But still she did not reply merely huddled up into herself and signalled for him to come to her. Gawain dismounted from the horse leaving him untethered near a tree where there was plenty of grass and close to the river where he could drink. Gawain followed the riverbank on foot towards where she stood, wondering to himself if its spring and source was from underneath or even the other side of the mountain as he couldn't see any fall of water on his side. He looked along the river to the cliffs shaped like grave stones and scoured them with his eyes thinking what a strange place it was. When he looked for the woman again she seemed to have bent down once more.

"Hello…," he shouted, but there was no answer, no motion only the stillness of the place. He turned back to his horse and called to him to remain there until he returned. He decided to run towards the place where the woman had appeared but on arriving at the spot he found only a huge, white rock, shaped like a woman bent double. Gawain prodded it and muttered to himself puzzled at how he could have imagined that the rock moved. He walked round it and studied it wondering whether his eyes were playing tricks on him. Glancing up he noticed high above the white rock towards the right of where he stood, a crevice in the cliff face just wider than the width of a man far up from where the river seemed to swell from the ground at the foot of the mountain. He realised that if he climbed onto the white rock he might be able to reach the fissure. He clambered, therefore, onto the back of the rock woman and scaled the cliff towards the crevice. All the while he could hear the sound of water falling seemingly from behind the mountain. As he reached the crevice, he looked down but the rock which had provided the platform for his climb was no longer there. He strained his eyes towards Gringolet in the distance who seemed to be grazing contentedly and then back to the empty place where the woman of the white rock had been. He realised that without this rock, there was no way back as he'd climbed too high so now he could only continue upwards through the crevice.

"This is a new adventure for the King," he thought out loud as he squeezed his way through the fissure and surveyed a precipitous ravine before him with the noise of the falling water in his ears. He edged around the cliff face until he was confronted by a torrential waterfall from high above him pouring down into a large lake far below. He reckoned that he had entered the ravine about a quarter of the way up. Looking higher, the cliff was sheer with no means to climb it and likewise on the opposite side although it was not quite as precipitous further up where he could discern a cave outside of which lay a large jet black rock similar to the white one on which he had climbed. There appeared to be no way up or a way across to that cave and the black rock. Looking towards the sky he could make out a dot circling above him which swooping down flew round and round coming closer and closer to him. The mighty eagle flew almost at him so that Gawain stumbled for a moment, before it swooped off into the ravine and eventually disappeared behind the waterfall. Edging carefully towards the falling water, Gawain saw that he too could go behind it to where the bird had disappeared and was now perched on a ledge at the rear of the fall. It was a magnificent royal bird with an intelligence shining from its eyes. Impulsively Gawain bowed to it and the eagle flew off having accomplished its task of showing him his way.

From the ledge where the eagle had perched Gawain discovered that behind the torrent there seemed to be a number of footholds protruding from the cliff which would enable him to climb up. He attempted his climb with the noise of the water almost deafening him. His hands and feet kept slipping but he reached a point where the gap between the water and the rock face narrowed. Here to his relief he found a steep pathway leading to the left which he followed, climbing higher up the ravine until the cliff widened out into a flattened area leading to the mouth of a cave on his side of the chasm, almost opposite the one he had earlier seen on the far side. This area was the only respite from the sheer cliff face which above it became precipitous once more and impossible to climb. Looking across to the opposite side of the ravine he saw some way above the cave with the black rock, a wooded plateau where there were some goats grazing, but looking up his side of the ravine, the mountain seemed to tower into the skies as far as he could see.

"From the height on the far side of the ravine," a voice said, "you will return."

"From up there?" he asked turning to find the woman of the white rock standing in front of the cave. He had no doubt that she was the woman he had seen earlier. "What is this place?" he asked. "What is the place from where you have come?" she asked in return. "The valley we call Cwm y Meirw," he replied. "This then is Ogof y Meirw and I am the guardian of the cave." "And up there?" he asked pointing up to the wooded plateau. "The Heights of the Meirw," she replied, "which will become known to you."

Gawain looked towards the mouth of the cave behind her. "Ogof y Meirw, the Cave of the Dead," he whispered. "You have arrived," she confirmed, "but do not be afraid. You are not to enter, not yet but you are to mark where this cave is and you will instruct someone who knows the way to it to undertake a solemn task when King Arthur needs it. Do you understand?" "I do, but will you be here to help?" he asked. "A bridge from the Heights of the Meirw will be the only way by which the King will be able to come. You need to cross to them now in order to return to him and undertake the task allotted to you."

Gawain scoured the rock face across the ravine but could see no bridge of any description or any means to build one so high up on the sheer cliff face of this hidden chasm. "But will you be here?" he asked again. "I'm always here," she answered. "Then I believe you to be Corwen, daughter of Idris," he said giving a respectful bow before enquiring further, "and the cave on the other side with the black rock?" "Ogof y Byw, the Cave of the Living," she explained, "to be guarded by one of Arthur's own." When Gawain asked who that might be and who lived in the cave, he was told that the cave was empty, that the black rock was waiting for the occupant and that Sir Gawain was asking too many questions. "So Black guards the Cave of the Living whilst White guards the Cave of the Dead and above the living are the Heights of the Dead," he mused to himself but was interrupted being told that all was as he perceived and as it should be. He decided that it would be wise to enquire no further nor to even think about it for the moment at least.

Gawain was suddenly distracted by the eagle once more flying above them until turning round he found that the woman had disappeared as suddenly as she had come and a large white rock now stood at the mouth of the cave where she had been. "I suppose I'll never know," Gawain muttered to himself, "but behind this rock must be the cave where the King will finally come to rest."

Gawain had not only found Ogof y Meirw, the Cave of the Dead, opposite Ogof y Byw, the Cave of the Living but had so far survived in doing so which no one to his knowledge had done before. His instructions were clear, he was not to enter the cave but return home with an understanding of how to reach the place when the time came, if of course, he was still alive himself. But it was clear that when King Arthur was to be brought to this, his last resting place, he could not be brought the way in which Gawain had arrived but rather from across the plateau above the Cave of the Living. It was evident also from Corwen's sudden disappearance that he was now meant to leave the place but as impetuous and curious as ever, Gawain decided to squeeze down behind the white rock and enter the kingdom of death, just to see what it was like.

Confronted by the vestiges of death he found that others had done so before since once in the cave's entrance he stumbled over skeletons, skulls, old bones, swords and knives scattered over the ground.

"Where are you going?" a voice thundered out of the darkness and he swung round to face Corwen in a rage of anger, no longer looking as an old woman but as a fearsome female warrior, her sword drawn, her shield prepared.

Gawain instinctively did as all the others had done before, he placed his hand on the hilt of his sword as if to fight but then, unlike his predecessors, he released it and knelt before her. "Forgive me, Corwen, but my duty is to my King, Arthur, favoured by your father, Idris, and I needed to see that all was prepared."

Corwen looked puzzled and asked him what he meant and Gawain explained that he could not have his King lying amongst all these bones and skulls. Arthur, when he arrived would need a place, a great Hall and Chamber suitable to his station. In the centre of which should be a stone bier fit for a King. Corwen fearful of her father's displeasure at her tardiness, replied that it would be so but remembering that Gawain had entered the cave without her consent lifted up her sword again in a rage. Gawain had regained his confidence and knowing that he could not defeat the god in arms, continued that he was pleased and grateful for Corwen's assurances but surely Arthur waking one day from his sleep of death to do, as prophesied, great things in the world, would be grieved not to see around him the remains of his friends treated with similar courtesy. So Gawain proposed that each of Arthur's warriors brought to the cave should have a niche hollowed out of the walls of the Hall where they could be laid to rest with their names engraved above them. Then when King Arthur awoke he would see his Knights sleeping near him and be comforted that they were treated with the respect that they deserved and who knew, at such times he might need to call on one or more of them to re-enter the world with him. Corwen considered this and agreed that it would indeed be a dishonour to Arthur to be surrounded by the scattered bones of his brave warriors and that all that Gawain had proposed would be done.

Gawain thanked her but she remembered once more his impudence in entering the cave without her permission and became angry lifting up her sword. Unflinchingly, he moved towards her as if to accept death at her hands but stumbled over a bone lying on the cave floor.

"Corwen," he called up to her, "what would happen if when Arthur, the favoured one of Idris your great father, is brought in solemn ceremony to this place, one of his retinue carrying him tripped on these scattered bones in the passageway causing Arthur's body to tumble to the ground? What an insult that would be to our King and to the honour of Idris his protector. Let me tidy this place and remove the bones of any not fit to lie in a cave such as this." Gawain moved to collect the bones and respectfully passing Corwen at the entrance of the cave, pretended to go to throw them down the ravine.

"Stop," she commanded, "have you no respect for the dead, even if they're not worthy of the cave which I guard?"

Gawain, with the bones still in his arms, apologised for the great wrong he had nearly committed, respectfully asking where the bones might be placed since he considered that the entrance to the cave should be cleared and then adorned with flaming torches so that the procession could enter unhindered and find its way easily to the great Hall where Arthur was to lie in his Chamber. Corwen beckoned him to follow her towards the waterfall where she commanded the cliff face to open revealing a charnel house which she said was a suitable place for Gawain to lay the bones next to the dismal remains of thousands of good people who had departed the world. Corwen's anger had subsided but Gawain thought it wise once again in front of such a deathly sight to apologise for his intrusion into the cave. She forgave him and instructed him to sit and observe whilst all he had suggested would be done. First she commanded the waterfall to cease its motion and be gone. Instantly the last drop of water fell to the lake beneath, then turning to the charnel house she raised her hands and called on the bones of the long since dead to reassemble and make their way to her cave of the dead. It was a grizzly sight to see the bones jostling with each other to find the ones that belonged to themselves rather than their former friends and then reconstructing themselves from toe bones to head bones before swiftly moving towards Ogof y Meirw. Once there they set to work digging and carving, hollowing out and building up, an army of death, foot soldiers all, working to make the cave fit for a King and his greatest warriors. There were no complaints, no laughter, no songs only the grinding and clinking of bones against each other and the occasional raising of a skeletal hand in apology as one bony foot accidentally stood on another or one tibia accidentally bumped into another. What a sight this was with Corwen directing the work just as Gawain had advised. Once finished she clapped her hands and the bones returned to their chamber and dismembered whilst she closed the cliff face around them and commanded the water to flow again.

Then she invited Gawain to enter Ogof y Meirw to see that all was as it should be. He entered through the passageway now illuminated by towering flaming torches, which lit the way to the great Hall and King's Chamber in the centre of which stood the stone bier where Arthur's body would be laid, the King's name and the following words carved around the base, "In this place lies Arthur, King of the Celts and the Lands beyond from which he will emerge as eagle or bear, as man or lion at the time of need."

Gawain turning to Corwen thanked her for her consideration. As she led him from the hall, the Knight took one last look at the hollows in the cave walls prepared for his companions, over one of which he saw etched the name, "Sir Gawain." He walked along the passageway in the fading light of the flaming torches and out into the sunlight where he breathed deeply, saddened by what was to come, yet joyful at being alive.

Corwen as if to make some final authoritative point had ensured that this time in being metamorphosed into her rock, she left no room between herself and the cave for Gawain to be able to return there. He surveyed the scene and puzzled what to do. There was no point calling across the ravine to Ogof y Byw since Corwen had told him that the cave was empty. He could see no way up the sheer cliff of the ravine from where he stood and knew that there was no way back to Cwm y Meirw for even if he were able to find the crevice he would not be able to scale back down the sheer cliff face into the valley where Gringolet grazed, without Corwen's rock to help him. He was stranded on a narrow ledge half way up a ravine, with no escape and yet with a command that he had to return to King Arthur and give instructions to one of the warriors, whose identity he did not know, to bring the King to this place when the time dictated.

He peered up high to where the eagle was circling again and across the ravine to the plateau on the far side. "Perhaps," he called to the eagle, "you might be able to help me again since I have no idea what to do. Corwen gave the impression of a bridge, but I can see none." He turned to the great white rock and knelt before it. "Corwen," he implored, "provide me a means to leave this place since you promised my time to stay had not yet arrived."

There was no answer but he saw the eagle fly across the height of the ravine in the direction of Cwm y Meirw. He followed the bird's flight until as a small speck, it disappeared from view. "What are you telling me this time?" he desperately asked the bird. "I cannot fly. There is no way up or down from this place and the cave itself is blocked by Corwen and as for the ravine, there is no way across. Do I pray? Do I plead? Do I beg?" He laughed to himself, "Something will happen. I just have to wait and see what it will be."

Night was drawing in and so he gathered stones and debris left by the skeleton workers and made himself a shelter. On the far side of the ravine he could see that the goats on the pastures of Heights of the Meirw were taking cover under the trees. "It's going to be a rough night," he whispered to himself as the weariness of his travels caught up with him and his eyes closed. In the middle of the night he woke suddenly thinking at first it was the storm that had raised him but soon realised that the ground was quaking and the mountain itself seemed to be moving. He rushed from his rough shelter, some of which had already crashed down into the chasm and backed towards Corwen with a wind now howling through the ravine, screeching its anger and frustration, seemingly determined to tear the mountains apart. "Is this how it's going to end?" he thought realising that another force had entered the chasm, a force which was as great at least as that of Corwen. He turned to the white rock and cried out,

"Corwen, Corwen, Corwen! Save me since Morgen of the Winds has pursued me here to this place to gain her revenge on my King. Please save me, save me!"

Lashing rain had now arrived but he said no more as with a terrifying crash he was hit by a branch blown from the Heights of the Meirw. He fell unconscious to the ground whilst the storm continued to rage. Morgen, dark and menacing indeed was searching to find and destroy him but was unable to see him lying against the white rock underneath the branches of a huge tree brought down across the width of the ravine by the force of her fury.

He was woken soon after dawn by a tugging at his tunic as a goat was foraging for food. The storm had passed and there was bright sunlight above the abyss. "How did you get here?" he asked the animal and looking around he saw that the fallen tree had wedged within the narrow part of the ravine forming a bridge which the goat had crossed. Looking upwards to the plain he could see Gringolet amongst the trees grazing patiently, the eagle circling above him. Gawain stroked the goat and the two of them steadily crossed over to the other side using the provided bridge. The eagle clearly had led the horse to the woodland pasture and would continue to watch over them until the horse and the rider were reunited. Once Gawain had crossed over the bridge the earth once more quaked and shook dislodging the tree trunk which crashed to the lake far below. Gawain looked back towards Corwen and shouted his farewell and thanks and then raised his hand in gratitude to the eagle as it flew away. The goat led him into the empty cave called Ogof y Byw where rocks had been dislodged from the mountainside leading up to the plain above. These he climbed, the goat going in front of him to rejoin its companions on the Heights of the Meirw. Gawain reunited with his horse, milked one of the goats before setting out on the journey back to King Arthur in the warmth of the sun. On leaving that place, he turned around to take a look at the rocky steps he had climbed from the cave below, but they had disappeared.

The first to see Gawain's return to King Arthur's fort from his adventures was his then servant boy, Tag. Each day that Gawain had been away, Tag had taken a position outside the perimeter boundary scouring the horizon for any sign of his master. The King had been told and had sent Gafallt, his dog, as a companion for the boy as well as to keep an eye on him. Some had complained that Tag should be working for other warriors whilst Gawain was away, but the boy was also looking after Gawain's possessions and the place where he lived and slept. So the King ordered that he should be left alone to watch and prepare for his master's return. Tag played with Gafallt keeping watch and preparing for his master's arrival. When the day came, Tag saw Gawain in the distance and as he'd planned whispered in Gafallt's ear that the time had come. The excited dog, however, had already seen Gawain for himself and was only too ready to run off to alert the King that there was news. The boy ran along the track towards his master, his eyes full of tears as he ran faster than he'd ever run before with Gafallt, having signalled his message, following after him as fast as his four legs would take him. As the King and Queen went to the gates the news spread that Sir Gawain was returning. Cornets sounded and drums rolled, flags were unfurled and crowds of people flocked out to welcome their hero home.

Tag reached Gawain and holding back the tears, looked up to the warrior as he caught hold of the horse's mane. "Welcome back," the boy beamed. "It is good to be back," Gawain replied, helping Tag onto the horse. "Come, you will ride with me into the fortress, for you are no longer my servant boy, but my loyal friend. Gafallt, my other friend," laughed Gawain as he leaned over to pat and fuss the dog, which out of breath but still excited jumped up on its hind legs towards them, "you too will accompany us as we ride to meet the King and Queen." And so they made their way through the cheering crowd until arriving at the gate Gawain halted and looking with love and loyalty towards the King and Queen, asked permission to enter the fort. "Enter with our joy," cried King Arthur, "welcome home, our Gawain has returned."

The stories of his adventures were recounted but Gawain kept silent about the visit to the King's last resting place, not knowing which warrior to trust with the information he had. The King watched him curiously, knowing that not everything had been said. Gawain was perplexed by the scrutiny but was waiting for a sign to be given. One morning he awoke to the sight of the eagle flying and watched it circling in the sky until it swooped down towards a path being taken by one of the warriors. He was the Black Knight, the one who presented Gawain with the helmet covered with jewels at the start of his quest. This trustworthy man put out his arm for the eagle to perch and stroked the bird gently before releasing it back into the skies. This was the sign that Gawain needed and giving his message to the Black Knight, Gawain completed his quest.

Following the civil war which brought to an end Arthur's kingdom, legend holds that the dying Arthur was placed in the care of three queens who took him on a barge across a lake and were seen no more. Who were the good women who accompanied the dying Arthur across the lake? Were they three royal queens related to him as some do hold or were they, as we may now surmise, three of Idris' daughters, not queens but goddesses? We cannot tell for certain and after so many years it is all too distant from us to be sure but when the barge that carried the King across the waters came to its landing place, they were met by the Black Knight who with six companions, carried the King on a golden pallet to the wooded pastures known as the Heights of the Meirw.

There they certainly saw that the three daughters of Idris had gone before them. A golden bridge had been erected across the ravine where on the far side Tanwen, Seren and Morwen waited. Below them at the entrance to the cave stood Corwen waiting to receive the King and his retinue. She lifted her arms and spoke words to the cliff face out of which appeared steps of marble glittering in the sunlight. Corwen then ordered the waterfall to still. Morwen, who stood with her sisters, called to the glistening blue lake below to raise its level to that just below the cave. It did so to the music of the heavens, instructed by Seren looking up to the bright sky. Then as Tanwen solemnly pronounced to her father that all was prepared, the three sisters disappeared from the sight of all but the King, who saw Idris with three of his daughters circled in the sun. The King knew that the cycle of his life was complete and his eyes gently closed. The Black Knight then commanded the six warriors to lift the pallet now holding the King's body on to their shoulders. With the waters glistening below them and Seren's music softly echoing from cliff to cliff, the King was taken across the bridge and down the steps to be met by Corwen who dismissing the Black Knight, led the cortege into the cave, along the passageway illuminated by the flaming torches and so into the great Hall and the King's Chamber where the pallet and its sad load was laid on the stone bier which had been erected. Corwen draped a golden cloth over the body and placed the King's crown at its head and his sword at his breast. The six Knights were then led to their named places of sleep amongst companions who had been brought previously from the battlefields. There Corwen left them closing the entrance to the cave and placing above it a large bell to be rung when the world was in such trouble that King Arthur was to be awakened or when there was a moment of such joy that the world should know.

The Black Knight as instructed had returned across the golden bridge to the Heights of the Meirw from where he saw the waterfall begin to flow again and the water of the lake sink back to the bottom of the ravine and the marble steps retreat into the cliff face. Seren's music reaching a crescendo filled the whole ravine as the Black Knight looked up into the skies from where a shaft of light shot out blinding him with an image too great for him to discern. He fell to his knees as a silence descended. Time passed and gradually as his sight returned, he saw that the bridge had dissolved into thin air and that he was alone. There was a rope hanging down the cliff side near where he was. This he used to clamber down to the place called Ogof y Byw, the Cave of the Living, outside of which there lay the black rock. Once he had arrived the rope fell down into the ravine below. Exhausted he lay on the rock and watched from across the ravine by Corwen, the Knight and the black rock slowly became indistinguishable as one. The Black Knight's metamorphosis accomplished, Corwen herself returned into the White Rock guarding Ogof y Meirw, the Cave of the Dead. White and Black, Black and White, Living and Dead, Dead and Living there in their rocks they wait silently unless disturbed by water, fire, the stars above or the actions of the world below.

NINE
THE RELEASE OF MERLIN

Morgen of the Winds, errant daughter of Idris, imprisoned Merlin in a tree in a forest sometimes known as the Wandering Wood. The curse that she placed upon King Arthur's friend and Counsellor, could only be lifted by a "young woman of life and death." How could such a young woman exist and who would she be? This was the dilemma for Idris which he determined to solve, as will be seen, with the help of his other daughters: Morwen of the Sea, Seren of the Stars, Tanwen of the Fire and Corwen of the White Rock. But the question was whether Merlin himself, if given the opportunity of freedom, would actually take it. His incarceration was not only one of the body but also of the mind. What was it like to be imprisoned in the tight bark of a gnarled old tree?

Imagine. You enter a confined space where you are just able to turn round, just able to squat down on the floor. It is totally dark unless painfully you force your head upwards to see the morning sun or the night stars but then your head sinks back into the blackness. Around you is the smell of wood, a sweetness that so overpowers you that your stomach heaves as you feel the gluttonous liquid of the oozing sap encompassing your whole body. You are closed in, drowning, suffocating in an endless memory of what you were and what you have become. There is no rest, no escape physically or mentally as the thick noxious sap seeps into every orifice and pore of your body, creeping between your fingers, your nails, the hairs on your head. The weight of the wood crushes down on your shoulders but you cannot die. Hunched up, squatting at the roots, permanently awake, you wait year by year, month by month, day by day, hour by hour, minute by minute. This was Merlin's prison, curse and torment locked inside his tree, alone with his memories.

Growing old is missing the ones you loved. For him the loneliness, the missing, the ageing was one in the unending labour of living a life without death. He longed to see those who had gone; the small seemingly insignificant singularities of a familiar face, of kind hands, of gentle posture. The slight incline of the head as attentive Guinevere listened to him or that tiny speck under the pupil of King Arthur's left eye which belonged to him and him alone. He desired to hear the sound once more of the King's voice calling, "Merlin, are you there?" for him to answer, "Yes, I am here, my King. How can I help?" "Come, I need you."

He would listen hard imagining, hoping he could hear Guinevere singing, the clarity of her voice so pure, but they were no more. King Arthur and Queen Guinevere had long since gone and though sometimes his mind played tricks giving him an occasional glimpse of them, he knew they were merely visions, dreams, chimeras, tricks, conceits prompting the imagination and exacerbating the pain, the missing, the loneliness. Growing old is loving the ones you miss.

Desperate in his loneliness, all Merlin had was the cruelty of memory and the prophecy of his release but gradually memory itself became as gnarled and all encompassing as the tree, convincing him that he deserved the punishment of his imprisonment.

Idris looked down on how the old Counsellor suffered and understood the torment Merlin endured. As a father he was ashamed of what his daughter Morgen had done to this good man and as a god he wished to release Merlin from his anguish of mind and body. But even this god did not have the power to lift the curse due to the malicious strength of Morgen's spell. That demanded the power of a young woman of life and death. So it was why Idris called a meeting in the heavens with his other daughters to set in motion a means to release Merlin. This is what they decided.

First, none of the daughters themselves could qualify as the young woman of life and death since they were eternal goddesses and as such were not young, human nor effected by death.

Second, there was no reason why they each shouldn't give birth through a relationship with a human if that is what their father would wish them to do.

Third, as Corwen was the guardian of the dead it would be unseemly for her to give birth. Therefore the responsibility would lie with Morwen, Seren and Tanwen.

Fourth, despite her responsibility to the dead, Corwen would be prepared to allow a female child who appeared to be dead on arrival at her cave, a period of recovery and growth under the care of Guinevere, who currently lay in Ogof y Meirw, the Cave of the Dead.

Fifth, Guinevere would be allowed two of her attendants to accompany her to nurse and care for such a child in Ogof y Byw, the Cave of the Living, until the child had grown and was ready to undertake the task.

How all this was to be achieved, however, would be dependent on the three daughters finding suitable partners on earth and each giving birth to daughters rather than sons and at least one of which might visit the Cave of the Dead or be deemed to have died and lived again. Idris found the matter of the sex of the envisaged babies amusing since he had already determined that the three would give birth to girls and as he was their god as well as their father, that is how it would be!

So it was that the three daughters scoured the world to find their male partners but they took care that in doing so Morgen would not see nor suspect them. Seren was the first to succeed. She saw a homely man named Alwain, who lived alone on a farm a distance from the Wandering Wood. She disguised herself as human. Alwain fell deeply in love with her telling her that she was a "goddess" without realising actually that was what she was. She gave birth to a daughter whom they named, Elan.

Next Morwen saw an honest man walking alone on a beach where the sea was as pure and clear as she wished it to be. His name was Meredith who unknowingly spurred on by Idris had come to this remote place so that Morwen could come from the sea to meet him. Meredith was watching a family of dolphins jumping in the summer sun when she appeared to him walking out of the clear blue water to greet him with her love. They lived in that remote place until their child, Elin, was born who Morwen immediately took back into the sea. Meredith fearing the child may have drowned was reassured by a promise that on returning to the beach every year he would be allowed a vision of the child as she had grown. For the rest of the year, Elin was nurtured on an island in the middle of the ocean and was given the gift of music.

Tanwen was the last to settle on her partner a huntsman named Victor, living in the East of the lands. They had a child named Elon, whom Tanwen asked Seren to bring up as a sister to Elan. Victor and Tanwen took the child to a place near where Seren and Alwain lived and delivered the baby to them. Victor returned alone and Tanwen returned to her work in the heavens.

Did Morgen suspect what her sisters were doing? Possibly she did. She certainly anticipated that there would be an attempt one day to release her prisoner. She therefore decided even before the internecine battle which brought King Arthur's kingdom to an end, that she would find a suitable human to guard Merlin's tree. The slaughter of the battle gave her the opportunity to find such a man. He was Sir Mordred who lay dying on the battlefield. She knew his foolishness and his role in helping provoke the war between the King and Sir Lancelot. She also saw him in better health as a suitable paramour for herself. So as he lay suffering from his terrible wounds she, disguised as a beautiful woman, approached him and whispered that she had the power to grant him life if he would be her lover. If he agreed he would live for as long as Merlin was imprisoned in his tree but if Merlin were to escape, she warned, Sir Mordred would be burnt to cinders. The dying man naturally chose for life and love and was comforted by the fact that the woman who spoke to him looked as lovely as the morning sun. She granted him full health and he was sent to live in the Wandering Wood where she would visit him.

It was there that they would wait for Idris and his daughters to make their move.

Years passed until Elin who had grown into a young woman of great beauty, was told by her mother, Morwen, all that had occurred and the quest that she was to undertake. On her birthday as custom dictated, Meredith came to the beach but this year instead of seeing a vision of his daughter, he found her waiting for him there with a task to perform. Meredith was to journey with her as her father and guardian to the Wandering Wood and in return she would each evening entertain him by singing to the accompaniment of the small harp which she carried over her shoulder in a red bag. Overcome with joy he looked out to the ocean for a glimpse of Morwen but saw only a family of dolphins to whom he called his thanks and his love for her.

So the two of them began their journey and each evening Elin played her harp and sang her songs keeping the two of them content and happy with each other in their quest. It was the sound of this music that a crippled old woman also heard and determined to find out its source. So it was why she made toward the place where Elin and her father rested not far from her home. The old woman on reaching there unseen, hobbled towards and sat behind a large boulder listening to the music which eased her wearied spirits. Having finished one of her songs Elin sensed that someone was close and called out, "Show yourself whoever you are."

Meredith jumped up looking around to see who it might be but Elin approached the boulder and once again commanded, "Show yourself whoever you are."

"How can I," came the reply, "for I am old and ugly, grotesque to look upon? You would not wish to see me."

"I would and I do," Elin insisted and with that the old woman hobbled from behind the boulder and showed herself.

"Oh you poor old thing," Elin instinctively said on seeing her.

"Poor but not old," the woman contradicted her. "I think I must be about the same age as you but for the ill fortune that I caused for myself and my family."

"And what was that?" Meredith asked as he joined the two of them.

The old woman whimpered that it was not for them to know but she thanked them for the music and went to return to her house.

"Stop, please," Elin pleaded placing a friendly arm on the woman's shoulder. "Sit down and tell us what has happened to you for I suspect that you are telling us that you are cursed."

The old woman saw the love in Elin's eyes which sparkled with her youth but once again declined and made to leave but Elin quietly said, "I'll sing you another song if you'll stay and then tell us your story."

"Please stay," Meredith interjected adding with laughter, "for Elin plays and sings so well that even the birds in the air stop to listen!"

The woman agreed and sat with her crooked back resting against the boulder. Elin played and sang a song of their quest which Morwen had taught her and once she'd finished she encouraged the woman to tell her story. The woman was overcome with the mystic healing of the song and said the music sounded as if it had come from the seas and the heavens which of course it had. So keeping to her side of the bargain she then began her story.

"Some children have pets, some have rabbits or cats or dogs but when I was a child I had a little bird. It had a damaged wing but I loved it more for that. I used to tell it that it would get better and learn to fly high in the sky where it would look after me, like that bird flying above us now."

The three of them looked up to see a large bird circling in the sky and then she continued. "We were happy my mother, father and me but one day my parents told me that I was to have a baby sister. They were so pleased but a deep resentment came over me. Whilst they were overjoyed I felt only jealousy and hatred. Who was this baby who would come between us? I would no longer be their only child and for me the happiness that I had known was lost for ever."

She paused shaking her head from side to side in anguish as she began to whimper and whine, her old face crumpling in despair. "How could it be that at such a young age I should throw away my love, innocence and life through such hatred? Soon after the baby arrived I committed an act so terrible that I deserved all that was to ensue."

"Keep calm," Elin encouraged, "I recognise something in what you are telling me. So be calm. I have come to listen and to help."

Elin looked to her bewildered father and signalled for him to ask no questions as the old woman breathing deeply, nervously continued. "The baby, a girl whose name was Elon, was healthy and beautiful and when she arrived my mother and father doted upon her. I could not understand where Elon had come from, a baby who now slept in a cradle next to my parents' bed. I did not like this new sister of mine and wanted her to go far away from my home. One night, whilst my parents slept I decided what to do. I crept over to the baby and gently lifted her from her cradle. I then placed her in a basket that my mother used and gave her a present to look after her. It was the little bird whom I loved. Perhaps I thought the baby's warmth might heal its wing. I crept out of our home. It was extremely cold but the moon was shining and I could see my way. I hid the basket containing Elon and the bird amongst rocks near a river not far from this place. I returned home and went back to my bed. No one heard a sound. In the morning I was woken by my mother's screams. My father rushed towards me to see if I was safe and seeing me cried out, "The baby has gone, our Elon has gone."

He picked me up and held me tight, he was crying just holding me with tears rolling down his face. "I know where she is," I whispered to him in fright. "My bird is guarding her. She'll be happy."

My parents looked at me in terror but my father became calm and asked me where they could find her. I started to cry but again gently he asked me where she was and I told them to follow me. We went out into the cold morning air and made our way towards the river. As we got closer I could hear my little bird chirping and felt sure that all would be well. My father ran to where I'd placed the basket but Elon was dead. My sister, the baby, was dead. She had died of the cold and my bird couldn't save her but her body had saved it, perhaps just for me."

The old woman was distraught and though Elin and Meredith were also distressed at her tale, Elin gently put her arm around her and urged her to continue.

"What happened next," the old woman cried, "was worst of all on that dreadful morning. A chilling wind had started to blow as I heard my mother say to my father, 'The child must be protected since she may be the one to lift the curse.' I did not know what she was talking about but my father seemed to understand and later in my life told me about the quest of Merlin's tree in which I now suspect from your song, you are both engaged. My father kissed my mother and then she lifted the basket with my sister and my bird still within it and walked down towards the river. I never saw them again but later my Father told me that she had followed the river to the sea where she was drowned. The winds were blowing fiercely as my father took me home. Although he was distraught he never chided or reproached me. He made food and as that day passed he played with me and was kind to me as he was for the rest of his life. That night the wind began to blow again and there was a loud knocking at the door. I hoped it was my mother returning but standing there in the howling wind was an old woman as crooked and disfigured as you see me now. She begged for food and shelter from the raging storm. My father welcomed her into the house and brought her to the table where I sat.

'So this is your little girl?' the old woman enquired.

He replied that I was his only daughter. At that the woman instead of sitting as invited bent over me and cursed me that I would grow from childhood to old age with no beauty in between."

"What?" cried out Meredith in anger. "She did what?"

Elin now told her father to keep calm as the old woman continued her sad tale. "And so it has been. Just as I reached the age of womanhood I became old and disfigured like you see me now. My poor Father in his distress at all that had happened, died soon after of a broken heart. Since then I have lived alone with my grief and my guilt and my old age."

"What can be done?" Meredith immediately asked his daughter. "What can be done? Your mother has powers. We should ask her what can be done?"

But again Elin reassured him as she sat with the old woman, asking, "Your name is Elan, is it not?"

"It is," the old woman exclaimed in surprise.

"And your sister, Elon, was not born by your mother but was fostered?"

"So she was," the old woman agreed in astonishment.

"Then know that I am Elin, daughter of this man here and Morwen of the Sea who told me of your story and instructed that when I should meet with you I should lift the curse of old age from you and tell you that your mother was Seren of the Stars of Heaven who will look down on us and help us in our quest."

She paused and then asked the old woman, "Do you wish me to do as my mother commanded?"

"I do," she replied incredulously.

Elin raised the woman to her feet and instructing her father to stand near her, she placed her hands on the woman's shoulders and proclaimed, "I Elin, daughter of Morwen, daughter of Idris our great progenitor, call on Seren your mother in the stars of heaven to lift this curse from you for which you have suffered for far too long. What was done was done and is forgotten now and for all time. Come back from the death like curse Morgen placed upon you and live your life as it was naturally intended to be."

With that the old woman fell towards the ground being caught by Meredith who looked into the eyes of a beautiful young woman. Evening had drawn to a close allowing the stars to shine lovingly as Elan, freed from the curse, was led back towards her home where they all rested for the night.

"So it was Morgen who posed as the old woman asking for shelter on that dreadful day?" Meredith asked his daughter as the two of them, now joined by Elan, continued their journey the next morning toward the Wandering Wood.

"Yes, Morwen told me all I needed to know and now Elan is with us on our quest."

"Two young women rather than one give us better odds of success," Meredith laughed, "and both of you have cheated death in one way or another."

As they journeyed along the track they were met by a man going in the opposite direction. They rested and ate with him. He informed them that he was going to find his daughter whom he had not seen since she was a baby but that it would soon be a significant anniversary of the day years ago he had given her to her aunt to look after. For it was this year that he had been told he should see her again and he was overjoyed at the prospect.

Elin and Elan looked at each other, fearful they knew who this man might be but it was Meredith who asked his name.

"Victor," the man replied, "and my daughter is named, Elon."

To the stranger's dismay, Elan burst into tears. Meredith went to comfort her whilst Elin took Victor off in another direction. There she broke the news to him of Elon's death as a baby and of how to protect Elan, Seren had walked down to the sea and drowned herself and of all that had since occurred. Victor was overwhelmed by all that he heard but the measure of this man was the concern he immediately showed for Elan to whom he returned with words of comfort. "Here," Elin thought, "is a just man and a virtuous human being."

After some time Victor told them that Elon's mother had been Tanwen and he recounted the story of how he had met her whilst he was out hunting. Three times she had appeared to him when he was stalking an animal he expected to kill. Twice he almost shot her with an arrow but on the third occasion she appeared from behind and caught him unaware. He fell in love and so it was that Elon was conceived. But now that he had been told his child was dead, he asked whether they might know the place where the gods would leave their loved ones to rest. Elan desperately insisted that Elon would have been lost in the sea with her mother and there would be no trace of her. But Elin, knowing perhaps the way of the gods better than her sister, advised him to go to the Heights of the Meirw and to Ogof y Meirw in the North of the land. He thanked them and went on his way in search of the Cave of the Dead.

From far above Tanwen saw all that was happening and what was to happen. Later that day, Victor found a horse tethered to a tree as if waiting for him and looking up to the sky he saw the great bird that had been seen by Elan circling above. The bird now flew Northwards with Victor following on horse back.

It was Morgen who first saw Elin and Elan making their way to the forest. Alerting Mordred to the danger she circled around Merlin's tree and saw that it was safe. The glade in which it stood and the mound opposite to it, she had contaminated with the spores of a deadly fungus, which could only be washed free by the foul waters of the lake. It retained its ancient spells calling out to a yellow mist of death to envelope all who dared to bathe. Morgen believed Merlin's prison thereby to be impregnable. Even if anyone succeeded by design or accident to approach the tree a ring of fire would burst out around it. The heat of the flames would be so great that no one could cross it, even if they dis-covered it in the Wandering Wood where all paths led to the foul smelling lake at the centre some distance from the tree itself. Morgen instructed Mordred to go out and meet with the travellers to find out who they were and where they were going and what was their purpose. He set out with alacrity meeting Elin and Elan just at a time when they found them-selves in difficulties. Meredith on trying to speed up the journey had veered from the track into what appeared to be a luscious green field but which had turned out to be a bog infested with snakes. Elin and Elan were trying to help him out as Mordred approached. He took charge immediately wrenching a large branch from a tree and holding it out to the sinking man. As Meredith was pulled clear a snake came with him which Mordred swiftly dispatched back into the lake with a whish of the branch.

So it was that Mordred endeared himself to the trav-ellers, introducing himself as Rerddom, a man of those parts who knew all the tracks and paths well, even those of the notorious Wandering Wood. They fell for his words and when he offered to be their guide, they accepted with-out hesitation. The snare was set. Merlin would remain entrapped in his tree of shame. Rerddom smiled to himself and charmed them on their way with stories of King Arthur and his knights.

Merlin from within his tree, sensed Morgen's presence when she spoke with Mordred. The old Counsellor had grown familiar with all the activity around him and all the noises of the forest and could distinguish the animals from each other and from any humans that were unfortunate to pass by his tree as they searched for an escape from the meandering paths. He knew that Morgen had set around him the circle of flame which would flare up consuming anyone who strayed too close. He would yell out to warn them but they would perish without hearing him.

The old Counsellor had even learned to distinguish between male and female and knew only too well the step of the man Morgen had sent to guard him. Often he would hear Morgen's cruel laughter as she circled around abusing him with her taunts. This was a wandering place, a negative world ruled by an evil which had become the norm of existence.

As the years passed so hope came and went like the wanderers on the paths until in his mind there was nothing left but a mental state of despondency and despair. Now, yet again, he heard Morgen telling her companion that women were approaching the forest but such news was too late. For Merlin, nothing he heard, nothing he thought, could even resemble hope but rather cruelly pushed him further into the inner darkness of his wood as he reproached himself for being imprisoned in such a way.

He had convinced himself that it was pride alone on that fateful day which had made him return haughtily towards Morgen's coven. It was his own pride, therefore, in himself, in his powers and in his decision to sacrifice himself that had brought him to such a state of total misery. In his conceit and arrogance he had tempted the witches to persecute him believing he would gain the renown and praise which had followed but which he could not enjoy. So it was that the deed that the wide world praised as one of courage, bravery, sacrifice and honour had become translated in his imprisoned mind to something worse than despair. In such a state he had determined that his infatuation with his own self importance which had taken him away from his King just at the time when Arthur needed him most, meant he should never be released into the world.

The suffocating sap of the tree had seeped into his brain, overturning his reason and condemning him to an eternal agony of being. Morgen had triumphed and there was no escape. Even if a woman of life and death could walk through the circle of fire, Merlin would refuse to be released. Morgen knew his thoughts and reveled in his torment. He was her prisoner in mind and body, her figure of sadistic delight. But Idris perceived all that was and determined a means to overcome the power his daughter had exercised. He had already summoned Corwen and instructed her to wake the King, who as an eagle, was flying once again in the freedom of the skies.

How foolish humans, or even half humans are to think that Seren, daughter of Idris, could have been drowned in Morwen's billowing seas, or that the life of Elon might have been dissipated by Morgen's winds however strong they blew. This was not so on that dreadful day when Seren and Alwain found Tanwen's child dead, lying beside a chirping bird with a broken wing. Might that not have been the clue? For love, care and kindness can often be found in the smallest of creatures and so it was with this injured bird, assigned to protect an innocent life. True it was that Elon died but as the spirit left the little one's being, it was held fast trapped between the bird's broken wing and its warm body. There Elon's life-spirit lay unable to be wafted away by the early morning air or even later by Morgen's howling gales. Seren sensed where Elon's life had found shelter and so took the bird and baby in the basket down the river towards the sea, calling on Morwen her sister for her aid. Deep into the waters she walked till Morwen washed over them all, returning the life-spirit to the child. Then in a moment they were lifted up high on a mighty wave which returned Seren to her rightful place amongst the stars. Above the earth's storms, the skies rejoiced that night as Seren with her precious load now sped towards Corwen's domain, the Cave of the Dead. From there the guardian of the dead directed them immediately to the Cave of the Living where previously she had sent Guinevere, whom she had woken and two attendants to nurse and raise a little child should such a one appear. The heavens sparkled with delight as Seren returned leaving Elon in that place of life so tenderly cared for by the former Queen and her attendants and guarded by the Knight of the Black Rock. It was in that Cave of the Living and its surroundings that Elon grew to womanhood. Some days she would ascend the steps that would appear from time to time within the cave to the plain above where she could be seen amongst the trees and pastures by Corwen below. Often she would take the bird with her and although it had been bestowed with a long life, alas its wing was still broken so the bird required her loving care.

It was on these Heights of the Meirw that Victor following the great bird arrived to find this beautiful young woman caring tenderly for a small bird.

"What have you there?" the rider asked.

"Why it's my little bird but it cannot fly."

Victor tethered his horse and took the bird into his hands, stroking it gently.

"You look after him well," he said. "He is a lovely creature. Where do you live?"

"With my aunt in a cave nearby," she replied asking, "why are you here for few ever come to this place unless in sadness?"

Victor, resigned that his child was dead, told her he had come to find his daughter's last resting place and asked whether her aunt might remember years ago if a dead baby was brought to the place called Ogof y Meirw?

"Why," the girl answered, "that cave is on the far side of the ravine which no one can cross but by Corwen's permission. But if you wait I will ask my aunt whether she can help."

With that the young woman went into the trees vanishing from his view. Victor surveyed the scene and thought how serene it all was. He looked across the ravine to where down below opposite him he saw a white rock behind which hung a large bell and wondered if that was where he'd find the cave where his baby lay.

"What are you doing here?" a gruff voice behind him demanded. Victor turned to see a Knight clothed in black, shield to the fore and sword ready, fiercely glaring at him.

"I am a hunter," Victor explained, "but I came here not to hunt or fight but to find my daughter whom I have lost."

"Who sent you?" the Knight stood his ground.

"No one sent me but the eagle of the heavens guided me on my way."

"And your name?" the guard demanded.

But before Victor could speak a gentle voice from the trees answered, "I believe his name is Victor."

"And so it is," replied Victor as he saw Guinevere and her maids approaching him from the woodland. Had he ever seen such majesty as now he saw at this moment of his life? Little could compare with such a vision and instinctively he went down on one knee and the Black Knight stood aside.

"Rise," Guinevere said, "for though once a queen I no longer am. You come in search of your child that was lost but that you have already found."

Victor stood up, "Already found!" he muttered.

"Victor, see here Elon your daughter whom the gods of nature saved on that day and night when all saw that she was dead."

Victor looked towards the trees from where Elon now, as from a mountain mist, walked towards him. "Is this the daughter of my dreams?" he asked. "Is this the one I sought, found and did not recognise?"

"My father, my father and so I am," Elon tenderly answered as they both embraced in the happiness of their meeting and the joy of her life.

"Let me look at you," he said standing back from her but still holding her hands. "So has death been cheated, my Elon, through your life in this place?"

"So it appears," she laughed.

"Look everyone," he shouted across the ravine. "Here is Elon, a woman of life and death, my daughter who has a great task to perform."

"And so she has," Guinevere confirmed.

The Black Knight sheathed his sword and lay down his shield and taking off his gauntlet shook Victor's hand and taking up his weapon again he disappeared into the trees. Victor looked around, "Where have the women gone?" he asked.

"Their task has been accomplished," Elon explained. "Look across the ravine. They have already returned to sleep in Corwen's cave."

Victor looking across thought he saw the figure of a woman where the bell hung but in a fraction of a second he realised it was only the large white rock that he had previously observed.

"There is little time," Elon told her father. "Your horse is rested and one has been provided for me. We must go from this place."

"Immediately to the forest, the Wandering Wood?" Victor questioned.

"Of course, where else since that is where my quest must lead."

The daughters of Idris looked on and Tanwen smiled to see father and daughter starting their journey together, the great eagle again appearing to guide them on their way.

Rerddom had ingratiated himself with his new companions who because of Meredith's rescue trusted him fully. They were foolishly open in informing him of the nature of their quest and he responded helpfully telling them that he knew the exact place where "Merlin's tree" grew, though he wondered whether there was any truth in the story. How naive they were in believing such a man. A time would come that their innocence on which he had played, would place them in great danger. But they were resourceful and would find an answer to most problems they encountered.

So it was that led by Rerddom, Elin, Elan and Meredith entered the forest following its criss cross paths as it pulled them deeper into itself. As night drew in, they decided to stop and take some rest. For the first time on their journey, Elin refused to play her harp and sing as she said that there was no peace within the trees to listen to her music. Meredith who was armed with a hunting knife Victor had given him, stood guard as the two women slept beneath a tree, with Rerddom some way off under another.

In the moonlight as Meredith watched the forest creatures foraging for food he saw a fox, its coat all wet, appear quite close to them. It moved towards Rerddom and almost touched his face. Rerddom immediately got up and climbed a tree to escape from a yellow mist encroaching across the ground following the fox and killing all in its path. Meredith yelled waking the women, shouting at them to climb into their tree and running over, climbed up behind them. The mist spread across the whole ground until it caught, enveloped and so suffocated the fox before retreating from where it had come. Meredith was furious with Rerddom for not warning them of the danger but decided to keep his anger and his suspicions to himself. Once on the ground they agreed to move on and find a safer place to sleep until arriving at a woodman's hut they rested till dawn.

A thick fog descended whilst they slept so in the morning they were forced to walk in single file following Rerddom at the front. "All paths," Rerddom called, "go to the lake but from there we can move away towards the gnarled tree that stands alone on the far side of a small glade. That's the place you seek."

It was an accurate description of the place but Rerddom was not perturbed in telling them since he had other plans that would mean they would die by the water's side. In the fog, the stench of the lake appeared to be getting worse, indicating perhaps that they were getting closer, when suddenly Elin cried out that she was trapped.

"What?" called Rerddom through the mist.

"My legs seem to be encased by the earth," she replied.

"So do mine," Elan called in panic.

"And mine," Meredith shouted.

"Oh no," Rerddom sarcastically laughed. "Don't tell me you've strayed on to the growing sands." As the three of them struggled to get free of the earth growing upwards around their legs, a soft breeze blew away the fog revealing Rerddom sitting on a rock well away from where they were stuck fast.

"What is this?" Meredith asked.

"Your end," Rerddom mocked, "since this is the shore where those foolish enough to enter the Wandering Wood arrive to meet with death. The earth is cursed and will grow around you slowly until you are smothered by it and sucked back down into its depths unless, that is, the smell of the lake doesn't kill you first. As for me, I've accomplished my task and there is nothing for me to do but leave you to your fate." He added with cruel humour, "I never like to see the end. It upsets me so." He laughed and then waited expecting that they might cry out to him or beg his help but Elin had signalled to the others that they should say nothing. Rerddom, shrugging his shoulders, left them to themselves convinced that Merlin's tree was protected and that these three would die on the lakeside like the others before them.

"What do we do?" Meredith asked once Rerddom had disappeared.

"I don't know," Elan sobbed. But Elin recalled that in one of the stories her mother had told her, King Arthur once escaped from a place such as this foretelling that someone else would come to purify the lake and the land of its curse. "We are the ones that can do so and still save Merlin," she concluded enthusiastically.

Meredith asked how the King had escaped and she replied, "Oh I remember that well enough. Quick, Elan start gathering as much of this bracken as you can reach and put it between the two of us, and you, father, and I will do the same. But neither of you touch the earth with your hands or you'll become stuck fast like a four legged animal."

They bent to gather the bracken but there was little around where Meredith was trapped and he could only forage for a few twigs. The women did better gathering a mound of bracken and twigs and leaves and placed them between themselves. Then just as in the old story, Elin found two stones and striking them hard against one another time and time again eventually she created a spark which caused the bracken to catch fire. The growing earth immediately retreated from around their legs and they were free. Elin taking her harp from its bag, handed it across to Elan. Then she thrust the red bag into the flames to catch fire. With Elin wafting the flaming bag to and fro in front of them, the two women made their way across the living earth toward Meredith to free him but he insisted that they should make for firm ground and find more wood, twigs and bracken and then come back for him since if the bag burned away, they would be stranded again.

Following his advice they reached solid ground just as the bag burnt out. Elin left Elan to keep watch over Meredith in case Rerddom should return and went to find fuel. It was as Elin was leaving that Elan called out to her to look at the lake. All three watched as a deer covered in a fungus from its legs to its head stumbled its way on the far side of the lake to the water and plunged in. When it re-emerged it was totally cleansed and ran towards them. But a yellow mist had now gathered over the surface of the lake and started to follow it, enveloping it before the creature could reach them, suffocating the poor animal to death. The yellow mist then returned to the lake.

"That was close," Meredith shouted with relief. "It could have been the end of me."

"It was the end of the deer," Elan said sadly as Elin returning to comfort her reassured her that she would not be away long. She took her harp from Elan.

"I can put it on the rock where Rerddom sat," she explained, "and where also you will be safe." She kissed her sister and called goodbye to Meredith before leaving them both to go into the wood.

Elin searched in vain for anything she could take back to burn as a path to Meredith. She could find nothing suitable on the ground as all the bracken and twigs had disappeared and when she tried to break some branches from the trees, they would only bend and not snap. Further and further she ventured into the forest circling the lake until eventually she reached a mound at the head of a glade. The wind blowing around her tired her out so she lay down sheltering behind the mound to rest. Opposite her was a gnarled old tree. Merlin sensed that she was there and called and called to warn her but she did not hear him for the howling of the wind and she fell asleep with a sound of laughter in the air, without even realising that Merlin's tree was in the glade in front of her just as Rerddom had described.

At dawn Elin woke crying out to find herself covered by Morgen's deadly fungus. Desperately she tried to pull it from her but it was deeply embedded in her skin. She shouted out for help but who could hear her in that desolate place, except Merlin imprisoned or Morgen laughing as the wind blew? The fungus was still encroaching, threatening to close Elin's ears, mouth, nose and eyes. Unless she acted quickly she would die in that place. There was nothing to be done except to head towards the water which had cleansed the deer.

Elan screamed when she saw her cousin, grotesquely stumbling out from the trees. "Meredith, Meredith, look at our Elin, look, look at our loved one. Oh Elin do not wash in that awful place."

Meredith who had been forced to sleep standing up with the creeping earth now having reached his waist, called out his love for his daughter, instructing her that once from the lake she must climb a tree as soon as possible. Both watched in desperation as Elin plunged into the water and disappeared beneath the surface. They waited and waited saying not a word in the silence of that dreadful place, scouring the lake to see where Elin might break free. There was no noise at all in the forest, no birds singing, no animals foraging, no creaking of the trees, no rustle of undergrowth, no indication even of their breathing. Sound itself had left this world. All watched in total silence for Elin to reappear. It was Morgen in the still of the winds who becoming suspicious made the first move to see what had happened. She did not have the patience of those who loved and ironically, began a course of action that would save them all. Breeze like, she gently approached the lake to peer into its murky depths to see where the young woman had gone. Had she drowned? Was she dead? Was this the one of life and death? Would she return to lift the curse? Despite all her stratagems to guard that place, was this the one who would defeat her? Morgen had begun to panic. Where was lazy Rerddom? Why was he not here? Was he asleep in that wooden hut of his rather than guarding over this man and woman who stared so at the black waters of the lake?

As she swept towards the water, she passed the rock where Rerddom had stood and unwittingly rippled through the strings of Elin's harp awakening it to start playing sweet music of its own devising. Meredith turned to see the strings of the instrument playing softly calling out to its mistress to come from the waters and so it was that Elin came.

"She's there," Elan called. "She's free! Meredith quickly looked to where Elan pointed. The sound of the music began to still the breeze as if fighting now to impose itself on this dreadful, wearisome place for too long ruled by uncouth Morgen.

"Quick, Elin, quick, quick, climb that tree, get away from what is to come," Elan urged.

"Climb, climb high," Meredith shouted. "Oh my daughter, beware of the mist. Climb!"

But Elin appeared to ignore their shouts for all she could hear was the sound of the harp and the music of the sea, where she had been nurtured. It was her mother's music, her mother's love calling her to stand firm and believe in her goodness. So it was that Elin stood cleansed of the fungus at the lake side. The yellow mist gathered over the lake's surface and rushed towards her. She did not run but rather bent down and confronted it, catching it in her arms and rolling it into a gigantic ball which she tossed back into the filthy waters from where it had come. For a moment the ball remained still hovering over the centre of the lake, until rising slightly in the air, it thrust itself down into the waters again as if attacking a deadly foe. The ball in its ferocity burst open and enveloped the lake from side to side, from its surface to its very depths cleansing it of its deadly evil. No drop found any place to hide but all was purged. With the work done and its resting place destroyed, the yellow mist disappeared into the sands of the earth releasing Meredith from its tightening grip. Morgen seeing all that happened rushed in the wind from that place to order her paramour to prepare for the next battle.

Elin ran across the sands to Meredith and Elan who both in turn ran towards her across the firm earth whilst the harp on the rock gently ceased its playing. "Morwen," Elin explained, "spoke to me beneath the water telling me to wait until summoned by my harp and instructing me in what to do once the yellow mist appeared."

"We thought you were drowned," Elan sobbed, "that you were dead but you are back to life. You are the one of life and death to free Merlin from his prison." Tears of fear and joy were flowing down her face.

"I do not know," Elin replied, "but we can wash ourselves in the bright waters of this new born lake and dry clothes have been left for us in the trees beyond, then our quest continues." They looked towards the crystal clear lake reflecting the blue of the sky above and then across the surrounding land which was covered in bright spring flowers.

"The daughters of Idris have been kind to us," Meredith said after they'd changed out of their wet and muddied clothes. "But more is to be done. Merlin is not free and our enemies are still around us."

"You are right," Elin agreed, "but our mothers will not fail us now." She then told them about the glade and the mound where she had slept. Meredith felt sure that this was the place where Merlin's tree stood just as Rerddom had described and where she must return to fulfil the prophecy. The time had come for Merlin to be freed by the woman of life and death and her identity and authority was to him now certain.

The forest looked different as they made their way through it, covered now in flowers with leaves appearing on the trees. But new danger lay ahead. They reached the glade to see Rerddom standing on the mound staring at an eagle flying low overhead which he coldly brought down with an arrow. Elan yelled as they watched the great bird at first lurch upwards and then fall into the trees at the far end of the field. Rerddom venomously turned to them, "So you've escaped and caused spring flowers to grow in the wood. I congratulate you but the bird as you see is dead and try as you might, you will not find a way to walk through fire.

Approach the tree over there and you and Merlin will all be burnt to death. I would enjoy watching what happens but the heat would be too intense for me. I'm going back into the wood for shelter."

With that Rerddom retreated into the shadows leaving the three of them looking directly at Merlin's tree.

"Are you there?" Elin called towards the tree but there was no answer.

She approached with the others following her but as she came closer she could hear sobbing.

"We have come to release you," Elin said.

Merlin from the tree replied, "The eagle, the mighty bird is dead."

"Not so," Elan reassured him. "I saw where the bird fell," and immediately she ran around to the far side of the glade in search of the eagle. Meredith and Elin watched apprehensively before Elin whispered to her father that the time had come to test whether she was indeed the chosen one. She moved closer to the tree.

"Stand back, stand back," Merlin implored, "you do not know what harm will come. I am encircled by a ring of fire. Look at the scorched earth before you where others have tried and failed."

His words came almost too late since Elin had placed her foot into the circle just as many had previously done. But with his words she retracted her foot quickly as the fire broke out with an intensity that made them jump back from the flames. Meredith dampened down Elin's burning shoe.

"It is not me. I cannot get to him," she said desperately. "I cannot breach that ring of flame. I am born of the sea, not of fire. What are we to do?"

The flaming circle started gradually to move towards the tree, inwards and then outwards back and forth as Meredith held his daughter assuring her that they would not be defeated. Merlin within his tree understood that something was different. All the others that had strayed too close, whether animal or human, had been destroyed and yet he sensed the woman's presence still and heard a man with her muttering. Could it be that this was the one of the prophecy? If so the prophecy should be damned for he would not leave this place, his just reward for the evil deeds of his life. Only the King could be a reason for his freedom and Arthur he knew was long since dead. He squatted down tightly near the roots, his head between his knees. These people whoever they were needed to depart, to go to the depths of the forest from where they would not escape. He did not know that the foul lake had been cleansed and that even his own tree was now in leaf.

On the far side of the glade, Elan found the great bird lying in some shrubs. He was caught fast, the arrow had pierced his wing and he could no longer fly. "I had a bird, much smaller but injured like you long ago," she whispered, "sadly it drowned but I will make you better." She tenderly lifted the creature into her arms and made her way back to Meredith and Elin.

"The great bird is still alive," she said, "look where the arrow pierced its wing but I will tend him and comfort him and maybe he will fly again."

Elin was hardly listening for in the distance behind her cousin, she had seen a sight so wonderful in itself that everything faded from her mind and yet raced back in a confusion of joy.

"Elan," she said, "give the eagle to my father and look where Victor stands, with the one whom I believe you wronged."

Elan perplexed did as she was told and saw walking towards her a woman as beautiful as the Fires of Heaven and next to her Victor, the huntsman whom they had met on their journey. The young women came face to face with Victor a little behind.

"Are you related to this good man?" Elan anxiously asked.

"I am his daughter," the woman replied.

"His daughter?" Elan questioned. "And my sister too?"

"Indeed that is so," the woman smiled as if the elements of earth and sky had met in a single, joyful moment.

"And what name do I call you?" Elan asked prompting the woman regally to reply, "I am Elon, daughter of Tanwen of the Fires of Heaven and of Victor, the huntsman here."

"And I am Elan, daughter of Seren, the sister who wronged you but who was forgiven by our cousin Elin, daughter of Morwen of the Sea that encompass the lands of the earth."

"Then daughters of the gods, let us embrace," Elon said, "and then fulfil the quest entrusted to us."

So as the circle of fire raged inwards and outwards getting ever closer to the tree, the three daughters embraced each other and kissed Meredith and Victor before Elon laughingly confided that fire could not harm the daughter of Tanwen. She then took the great bird with a damaged wing from the arms of Meredith and wrapping it in her sleeves, she walked through the circle of fire and untouched by the flames, stood before the tree.

"Merlin, Merlin," she called. "Step from the wood of this foul place and enjoy your freedom."

But Merlin remained silent.

She repeated her command but Merlin would not listen as the great bird in Elon's arms began to struggle. Once more she cried out her command but still silent Merlin refused to be purged of his grief. The great bird had now struggled free from its confines and stretched its wing towards the heat of the flame which healed the wound allowing the eagle frantically to fly round and round the tree.

Elon entreated, "Merlin be free, step out from the wood of the tree," but nothing happened. Merlin made no move. From outside the burning circle Elin and Elan pleaded, shouting out to Merlin but he did not respond. Round and round the eagle continued to fly frantically as the flames grew closer and closer, endangering the tree itself. Soon it would be consumed. Morgen had determined that this would be the final act, the end of all that had been in those days of Arthur's reign. Elon called to the bird, "He will not listen to me, even though I am the one, come settle, settle and be as you were and as you are, the key to his freedom."

She held out her arm and the bird perched upon it. From outside the circle, Elin and Elan, Victor and Meredith now saw King Arthur standing with Elon before Merlin's tree. The King with an authority as great as the gods themselves called out,

"Merlin, are you there?"

And the old Counsellor replied,

"Yes, I am here, my King. How can I help?"

"Come, I need you," the King quietly commanded. The bark of the tree unlocked releasing Merlin who knelt before his King and the woman of life and death who had walked through the circle of fire.

It was then that those looking on heard a sound coming from many miles away as Corwen rang the mighty bell to announce to the living and the dead that Merlin was free to return to those he loved.

"This truly is the end of Morgen's curse," Meredith shouted out aloud but the errant daughter had not finished, for the breeze turned to a wind and then to a gale which spread the fire into the Wandering Wood to set the whole forest ablaze.

"We will wait here," Victor advised, "until the fires die down but look, look where the King, Merlin and my daughter fly as eagles from this place."

And so it was that they saw the three within the ring of fire now as eagles take flight towards the great mountain called Cadair Idris, where some say they still can sometimes be seen, circling above when they are not resting with the Meirw.

All but a stump of Merlin's tree was soon consumed by Morgen's fires but mighty Idris, who had seen it all, sent a torrential rain to quench the flames of the forest as his malignant daughter fled in fear of her father's wrath. And so the four companions of the quest walked freely from that place, Elin retrieving from the rock her harp, untouched by the flames, before they passed the burnt out hut where Rerddom, foolish man, had taken shelter.

"So Rerddom is dead," Elin coldly stated as she looked at the cinders of that place.

"I doubt it," Meredith replied, "for evil ones lie and evil itself will never die. In the end good has to endure, constantly healing the wounds inflicted."

Below the Heights of the Meirw the ringing of the bell had ceased and Corwen had returned to her station as the White Rock. But across the ravine, a little bird flew from the Cave of the Living to the world beyond.

TEN

CROSSING THE RAVINE

It is said by some that King Arthur is not dead but rather sleeps and so can be woken when his people need him. Stories tell of him appearing at important times in history and of his warriors roaming the world under various guises awakening him and those who rest with him when the world needs him most. This last tale tells such a story which occurred a few years before the outbreak of the Second World War in Europe.

In 1936 Curnan Reilly from Boston, USA read a newspaper article that a shepherd boy had claimed to have discovered the cavern in which King Arthur and a number of his Knights were allegedly buried in North Wales. It was only a short report which indicated that the claim was not being taken seriously but it fascinated Reilly who had a deep military and historic interest in Arthurian tales. Nevertheless Reilly thought little more of the claim until a man appeared at his door who introduced himself as Dafydd Myrddin originally from Wales but now a U.S. citizen. Reilly immediately became curious since "Myrddin" is the Welsh form of Merlin but further the stranger had a dog with him which he called Gafallt, the same name given by King Arthur to his dog so many centuries before. The stranger explained that he had seen Reilly in a bookshop and again in the nearby library searching for books on Arthur and he wondered if Mr Reilly had read of the shepherd boy's discovery and if so whether he thought there might be any truth in it.

Reilly invited Myrddin into his home and a friendship developed between them over the ensuing weeks as they recounted to each other many tales about King Arthur but the stranger kept coming back to the article in the newspaper and the myth that when the world was at peril, Arthur would awaken from his sleep and with his Knights would re-enter time and do what they could to help the forces of good. Myrddin went on to say that in his view the world at that time was in extreme danger from the rise of Hitler in Europe and perhaps this was a moment when the ancient King could be awakened by the ringing of the great bell which Corwen, the goddess and guardian of those that slept, had allegedly hung at the entrance to the place known as Ogof y Meirw, the Cave of the Dead, for that purpose.

Reilly showed scepticism over what he was being told but Myrddin convinced him that if a boy had found the cavern, which itself had always been considered mythical, might he not have seen the great bell hanging there and if so, should it not be rung at least to see what would happen. He went on to explain that he, Myrddin, was far too old to test this out for himself but wondered whether, Reilly a younger man, might like the opportunity to do so. It took some time to persuade Reilly but Myrddin was insistent, offering to pay for the passage to Great Britain on the return leg of the maiden voyage of the luxury new ocean liner, the Queen Mary and to compensate Reilly for all his expenses and inconvenience. He even produced the first class ticket for the expedition and told Reilly that on his arrival at Southampton he would be met by Gafallt, his hunting dog, who would help him find a way to the place called the Heights of the Meirw from where the boy reported he had seen the cave.

Much to Myrddin's delight, Reilly eventually agreed and at that was given a sealed envelope with an instruction not to open it until it was needed. When Reilly questioned how he would know if it were needed, he was informed that he would know. Reilly laughed and Myrddin smiled. It was as if they had known each other for many years. The adventure proper began with him arriving in New York to board the Queen Mary which looked resplendent with its three funnels gleaming against the sky line. There was fervent activity, laughter and jostles as Reilly mounted the gangway and boarded. He found his cabin to be more than satisfactory and the facilities on the decks, in the panoramic bar and in the lounges to be not only fit for use but of impressive comfort. In his cabin there was a note from Myrddin reassuring him that Gafallt was already in England and would be waiting for him and that they were to journey by train, the tickets enclosed, to a small hamlet, Penmaenpool, which lies beneath the mountain Cadair Idris, of which so many tales are told. The letter ended with a warning that Reilly should take care, since evil forces were at large, prepared to do anything to prevent Reilly accomplishing his mission and warned that they already knew his surname. Curnan Reilly had so far been impressed by all he had heard from Myrddin and decided that on the ship at least, he would instruct the crew to call him Curnan, or Mr Curnan as Myrddin advised in the note, where he'd added incomprehensively to Reilly that in any case it was a more appropriate name for him.

Blasts from the massive horns of the liner kept sounding periodically until the voyage began, sailing past the Statue of Liberty and out into the Atlantic Ocean. For the first two days nothing untoward happened and Curnan made the acquaintance of a number of people on board and in the restaurant and in the sumptuous art deco lounge but on the whole kept himself to himself. It was on the third day that the bridge issued a warning that a storm was predicted that night. It was on that day also, that Curnan overheard some passengers talking excitedly of the rumours already developing that strange incidents had been reported about the ship as it was being built and during its maiden outward crossing. In short, they were saying that from its very first voyage and even before, the Queen Mary was considered to be haunted.

Curnan thought this to be utter nonsense but was uneasy as the waves started to rise with the coming storm and so decided to go to his cabin. There Curnan lay for a while looking at his watch, seeing the seconds ticking past. Outside the storm was gathering momentum making the ship roll quite dramatically. Curnan did not have the best of constitutions and peering at the watch did not help his stomach. Feeling sick, he thought that his cabin was not the place to be and that he'd rather head for the deck to get some fresh air into his lungs. Even to be able to see the ocean in the storm would take his mind off his nausea and so donning his raincoat and an appropriate hat, he ventured out and made for the deck.

He was soon disappointed as the deck had been roped off with a notice informing everyone that it was too dangerous for passengers to proceed. In reading this his nausea increased and not wishing to return to his cabin he decided to make for the bar for a glass of brandy or rum which might calm him. The liner was tilting this way and like a drunken man he entered the opulent Observation Bar with its panoramic window. It was now almost three a.m. and he supposed that he would be the only passenger out of the cabins but in the bar were a man and a woman with their backs to him, huddled in deep conversation over their drinks. No bar steward was on duty but there was a prominent notice informing passengers that in keeping with the tradition of the sea, a bottle of rum was available for a shot or two free of charge for any passenger that had ventured out in such conditions. Curnan, even though feeling nauseous, thought this hugely funny as he went to the cupboard marked rum. Whilst the rest of the bar was closed, this cupboard still had the key in its lock. Inside, as promised, was a very large bottle of rum together with pewter "shots". He poured one and drank it back before pouring another and ignoring the couple, went across to the window to get a closer view of the sea which was swelling high in front of him. The huge waves were breaking over the decks but the liner was coping well and he wondered why he'd been so foolish as to leave his bed only to come and view such a storm. As he watched, sipping his drink a calm descended and the water stilled allowing him to look out to the distance illuminated by the ship's lights, the best modern technology could devise. The storm seemed to have stopped as suddenly as it had begun with the moon now allowing him to see a vista of calm water which appeared to be pulling back from the furrowing liner.

"Have you seen what's happening?" he called to the couple but they ignored him. Turning back and looking towards the ocean he saw an enormous wave gathering from the retreating water ahead of the ship. It was rising higher and higher from the sea to frightening proportions. "Oh my goodness," he cried, "look what's happening!" Still the couple didn't reply. Instinctively he was moving away from the window as something made him stop, the perpendicular sheet of water brilliantly illuminated by the moon and the ship's lights was now moving faster and faster towards him. The ship was keeping its course but the wave was acting as a gigantic mirror reflecting the huge liner approaching it. The RMS Queen Mary was heading for certain destruction and Curnan could see it happening down to the very last detail. He watched the Captain and officers on the bridge steering the course with a steely determination. The Captain had a strong face of authority which seemed to merge with the image of the full moon captured in the towering wave. This man, he knew, would broach the wave and ride the storm but he was not the Captain that Curnan had seen on board over the previous days, indeed he looked a little like Myrddin. He put that thought to one side since he was enervated by the sight. In the impending wave he could see beyond the Captain's bridge the first of the three funnels and he could see himself in the observation bar, watching, looking, searching for an answer. How scared he looked and yet how confident. But there was something else in the image caught by the wall of sea that was not part of the reflection but entirely different. He could see in the risen water images of destruction not of the liner but of towns and cities where people were suffering in terrible, horrific ways. They were being crushed by falling masonry, by fire and by a blinding light that appeared instantly to eliminate them. Curnan turned away and looked toward the couple at the bar.

"Have you seen all of this?" he cried out to them but they only laughed to themselves without looking at him. He turned back to the wave which was almost on top of the ship. The Captain was all that he now saw, the piercing, intense reflected eyes peering directly at Curnan from the wave as he grappled with the storm. The image blurred and another appeared. The wave was on the verge of enveloping them but Curnan saw clearly a vision of Merlin surrounded by a ring of fire. Ridiculously the stories of the old Counsellor imprisoned in a tree came into his mind as the wave hit the liner and all Curnan could think about was Merlin's suffering as he heard himself cry out, "Merlin! Merlin! Merlin!" He was thrown backwards across the room, landing in pain at the foot of a table. He put his hand to his neck which was bleeding, his eyes were blurred forcing him to focus but there standing over him, raging at each other were the couple from the bar.

"Why didn't you silence him? Why did you wait?" the woman was shouting at her partner who grotesquely staring into Curnan's face yelled back at her, "Why didn't you? How did I know who he is or why he's come?" Curnan was still conscious and recoiled from the sight of the filthy, germ ridden old hag with running sores down her face, oozing noxious mucous from her eyes, nose and ears. To his horror he saw that her forehead was split in two as she glared down at him. Next to her was a tall, thin, stooping companion with stained clothes and pock marked face, his obsequious, false smile revealing decaying yellow teeth. Their very presence was threatening, abusive, offensive, frightening as the split in the woman's head seemed to widen the closer she moved towards him revealing bloodied knots within. Curnan screamed, recoiling at the sight and at the dreadful stench that surrounded her. Was he still in his nightmare? At the sound of his yell, the two revolting figures changed into a dignified woman advanced in years but comely in appearance and a young man, well groomed and wearing an immaculate tailor made suit. They tried to help him up, showing apparent concern for him as a voice from across the room bellowed out, "Leave my ship." The couple looked in the direction of the door. "Leave my ship," the voice commanded with such authority that to Curnan it seemed as if the tables and chairs would obey him. Then quietly, he saw the shadow of a man coming closer to where the couple stood. The voice commanded them for a third time to leave the ship and immediately they were gone as if they had evaporated into the air. The Captain of the Queen Mary leaned over and stretched out his hand for Curnan who grasped it and stood up rather unsteadily.

"Who were they?" Curnan gasped. The Captain looked across to the observation window. "The storm has died down," he said reassuringly. "What a vessel! That last wave must have been at least ninety feet high and we've survived with little damage. It was a freak occurrence. Maybe those two were behind it." He glanced around the room making sure that they were gone. "It won't happen again, not this year at least. Six inches more and we might have been lost, but we're not. Are you fit, Mr Reilly?"

He smiled in saying Curnan's real surname as if it amused him slightly. "Yes, Captain, thank you," Curnan replied still perplexed. "That's good. You'll be able to complete your journey without any further mishaps." "I hope so," Curnan said, realising that the pain he'd felt had completely gone. "Good, the sea will be back to normal by morning and people will enjoy the rest of their voyage and we'll get you to dry land, so that you can continue your quest, these fascists won't wait for ever." "No," Curnan answered confusedly still wondering whether he was awake or asleep and if this was the real Captain or not. Whichever, as the Captain went to leave the room, he turned to Curnan and asked him not to say anything to the other passengers about what had occurred. "Who was that woman?" Curnan asked in horror thinking of the vision and recalling the smell. "Morgen," the Captain simply replied. "And the man?" "Her companion," the Captain laughed. "He keeps popping back to life every now and again but he runs when you challenge him. Mr Curnan there is nothing more to worry about. It's all over for now," he stressed in his kind, comforting voice, repeating, "all over for now," as he left the room.

"Morgen," Curnan whispered to himself, "and her long since dead companion. What business is going on here that I have got myself into?"

The RMS Queen Mary provided no further visions for Curnan who when the liner docked in Southampton was greeted by Gafallt just as Myrddin had promised. Master and dog travelled as instructed to Penmaenpool where they stayed at the Inn near a wooden toll bridge, where on the first night Curnan was sure he saw the image of King Arthur looking over its side at the swirling waters beneath. But no sooner did he see it than the vision faded and so he said nothing, not even to Gafallt.

Early the next day, he was told that a boy was asking for him in the lounge who on their meeting told him that he was the one mentioned in the newspaper article. When questioned why he had come to the Inn to find Curnan, he replied that he had been instructed to do so by an elderly man who did not give his name. Curnan questioned further and suspected Merlin to be the man. But all this was conjecture and we need to get to the facts.

Arrangements were made by Curnan with the boy's parents for the boy to lead him to the place he called the Heights of the Meirw, from where he had seen Ogof y Meirw on the other side of the ravine. They insisted that the boy should not attempt to cross the ravine which he had described to them but only lead Mr Curnan to the place.

So the shepherd boy, dog and Curnan travelled North from Cadair Idris, passing the beautiful lake at Bala and onwards towards the Heights of the Meirw covered now in thick forest, following the same route once taken by those who carried the body of the King to his last resting place.

The Heights were an untamed, thickly overgrown inhospitable place. Gafallt showed no fear as he led the tortuous way through, the shepherd boy at his side whispering to him as the dog meandered his way to their destination. "What's happening?" Curnan asked only to be told that the dog was following the boy's scent from the previous time he'd been there when becoming lost he'd aimlessly wandered about back and forth until he'd arrived at the ravine by accident. Curnan now understood why Gafallt had been given to him. There had never been nor ever would be such a good hunting dog as Gafallt and here the dog, or his distant progeny, was searching out the route towards possibly the most hidden or secret valley on earth.

Occasionally Curnan heard the sound of twigs snapping and rustling behind them or near them and once he thought he caught sight of Morgen watching from behind a tree, her companion a few yards off, behind her. "Get off my ship," he called out with authority and "Get out of my forest," and they disappeared immediately.

At last with arms, hands, faces and bodies bruised and cut, the shepherd boy announced that they had arrived. Curnan came out of the trees to a shout from the boy to stop where he was, almost teetering on the edge of a ravine. "I've done my job now, sir," the boy said, "and will go back as my parents told me." "Yes, yes," Curnan agreed absentmindedly as he looked across and down the ravine to where the distant waterfall, which he could hear, tumbled down vertically to a lake far below. "There's the cave," the boy pointed across the ravine to the entrance of a cave behind a white rock shaped like a kneeling woman. "Why do you think it's the Cave of the Dead?" Curnan asked. "Because the Black Knight told me," the boy replied. "And who is he?" "I don't know but he was standing just where you are now and once he'd told me, he disappeared." Curnan thought for a while before asking the boy if he had told anyone else about the Knight. The boy replied that he hadn't as no one would have believed him. "So I just said that I'd found the cave and a bridge leading to it." But Curnan looking around said that there was no bridge. "No," the boy answered, "and no one has been able to find this spot since except for me and the Black Knight of course." All the time the boy had been looking at Gafallt and suddenly added, "May I take the dog with me?" Curnan came out of a reverie and saw the boy looking up at him. "Of course," Curnan told him, "but, in case all does not go as I hope, I need to write a note for Gafallt's collar and when someone comes to collect him, tell the person to read it." With that Curnan scribbled the note and placed it in a pouch on Gafallt's leather collar, before patting the dog and shaking hands with the boy bidding them farewell.

They were soon out of sight amongst the trees with Gafallt following the scent for their return but the boy, thankfully, had other ideas and if he had not, we would never have known what happened next. Quietly the boy and dog crept back close to where Curnan still stood staring across the ravine. Gafallt lay down by a tree which the boy climbed to get a better view.

Curnan remained standing for some time before he sat down on the edge with his legs hanging over. From his pocket he pulled out an envelope which he tore open and read the contents. He looked along his side of the ravine then easing himself up from the edge, he walked back into the forest searching the area not far from where Gafallt lay. The boy was anxious in case the dog barked but alert Gafallt remained quiet. Curnan walked back out of the forest to the same place as earlier and once more perused his side of the chasm obviously looking for something in particular. The boy inched his way along the thick branch until he was hanging over the chasm and looking back saw that Curnan had identified a place where a root of one of the trees protruded from the side of the cliff. This was marked with a large letter "M". Curnan edged along to the point where he stood directly above this protrusion and turning his back on the ravine, he walked into the forest counting ten trees in a direct line from it. The boy scrambled back along his branch and across to another allowing him a better view of Curnan now at the tenth tree. Curnan bent down and rummaged in the soil until he found a lever which he attempted to pull but it would not budge. Stepping over it, he straddled it and bending down again with both hands pulled and pulled the handle vertically, until suddenly it gave way throwing Curnan backwards onto the ground. Instantaneously, the boy crouched down across the bough of the tree as from the other side of the ravine two shining bolts roared towards him one of which buried deep into his tree with such force that he was thrown off his branch onto the ground. The second embedded itself in a parallel tree close by. Gafallt merely observed as if he had seen all of this before and then getting to his feet he silently went further into the forest. The boy picking himself up, followed the dog back to where Curnan now stood, who catching hold of the boy asked him what he was doing.

The boy explained that he'd promised not to cross the ravine but that didn't mean he couldn't watch. Curnan laughed and agreed that he could stay. Together they went to the two trees where the bolts had lodged and found attached to them a rope ladder which now hung as a bridge across to the other side. "How did you know about the lever?" the boy wanted to know. "A man gave me a letter which I was to read when I didn't know what else to do. As I was totally perplexed I read it and was instructed to look for the protruding root marked with the first letter of his name and count ten trees back." "And now?" the boy asked excitedly. "The letter told me who I really am and the role I have to play. I need to cross the bridge and wake the King and his men, by ringing a bell at the entrance to the cave."

As Curnan explained Gafallt started to circle round and round his master until when told to sit the dog ran into the forest with Curnan and the boy following calling for him to stop. But Gafallt knew exactly where he was going and stopped at an old tree with a hollowed out trunk inside of which Curnan found an army uniform, complete with pistol and ammunition, socks and boots.

He changed his clothes and with the shepherd boy and the faithful dog watching, returned to the rope bridge. It had no sides, no wooden struts, merely horizontal cords between the two long ropes stretching the width of the abyss. Curnan grabbed hold of one of these rungs and with his arms above his head, he swung suspended above the abyss moving his hands from one rung to the next. It was painfully slow work, hanging in mid air, his arms aching and pulling at his chest and lungs so that he could hardly breathe whilst sweat poured down his face and body but slowly his determination and his earlier service in the U.S. marines meant that he succeeded in reaching the far side. Perching himself on the narrowest of ledges, he signalled to the boy to unleash the rope bridge from the bolts in the two trees, which once done allowed the ropes, still being held fast on Curnan's side, to drop down into the ravine. Now Curnan descended the chasm on what had become a rope ladder until he found himself a few feet above a white rock onto which he dropped with a thud. Everything then happened so quickly. The rock disappeared, Curnan falling to the ground stared up at a fierce looking woman, clearly a mighty female warrior with a sword drawn who he knew from his reading must be Corwen, daughter of Idris and guardian of the dead. Meanwhile behind her across the valley, he saw a massive spider had stirred which first pumping itself up onto its legs, now catapulted itself into the air towards him. Curnan had no means of escape except towards the sealed mouth of the cave where the boy from the other side of the ravine could see the large bell hanging and started shouting, "Ring the bell, ring the bell." Curnan ran towards it and jumping up caught the bell rope with such force that he started swinging on it thereby ringing the bell. The deafening sound reverberated into the chamber, the booming echoing around inside the mountain before rumbling out with a blast of air blowing away the sealed entrance and filling the whole ravine. The black eight legged spider hurtling through the air was blown back the way it had come smashing into its side of the ravine where it slithered back to its ledge. Corwen now stood back from the cave entrance allowing a troop of soldiers all dressed in uniform to march out of the cavern. Curnan, who had hung onto the swinging bell, dropped down amongst them joining their ranks so as not to be seen by Corwen and thereby made his escape. The troop headed for the rope ladder and started to ascend and on reaching the narrow ledge where Curnan had perched earlier, the first kicked at it hard with his foot releasing two further bolts which shot out across the ravine.

Corwen was enraged that Curnan had rung the bell without her permission and although, by its ringing, those required for the quest had left to do whatever good they had been called to do, she was determined to find the interloper and so was counting the soldiers as they climbed. Realising that there was one more than the number that had been sleeping in the cave, she rushed towards the waterfall and caused it to stop and then opening up the charnel house beneath it ordered the bones inside to find the intruder who had dared to ring the great bell. "Do not wait to find your own bones, but assemble and pursue," she commanded. At that different bones united with others so that arms became legs and legs arms and a mixture of the two. Skulls positioned themselves where the pelvis should be or in the middle of broken rib bones. It was chaos as the bones assembled themselves in all kinds of configurations. The most frightening was one which joined horizontally together end to end three back bones with leg and arm bones hanging down from it so that it looked and moved like a grotesque giant centipede. This skelepede had a skull at one end looking forwards, one at the other end looking backwards and in the middle two skulls one at either side constantly swivelling but looking in opposite directions. It ran and scrambled at great speed after the soldiers up the sheer cliff face towards where the last of the troop including Curnan were now hanging from the rungs of the new bridge. As the very last soldier swung below onto the bridge, he hacked through the ropes of the hanging vertical ladder, plunging it down the mountain side, together with some of the pursuing skeletons. The skelepede and others in the army of bones continued to scale the cliff face and clambered onto the new bridge. Once there they experienced difficulty crossing with a number immediately falling through the rungs but the skelepede stretched itself across the bridge covering almost half of its length and allowing its bony companions gingerly to walk over it towards the place where Curnan and the last man hanging underneath were pulling themselves across by their hands. It was at this point that the spider from the other side of the ravine, having recovered sufficiently, decided to pump itself up to take flight again, this time towards the bridge. Up and down, up and down on its eight hairy legs it pumped until it took flight towards the bridge which was sagging with the weight of the number of weird bones crossing the skelepede above, together with the last of the cave's troop crossing underneath hand over hand. As the pumped up giant black spider now hurtled close to Curnan, the man behind him, the last to cross, called out, "Know you not who I am?" and with that the spider altered its course so as to go higher and then came down from above onto the unsuspecting skelepede, whose skulls looking to the front, behind and the side had failed to see its approach. With the extra weight of the massive spider, the rope bridge unable to support the burden, snapped sending its Ogof y Meirw end down into the ravine and expelling the skelepede and all the bones clambering over it into the lake far below. The spider caught on to the end of the ladder which was still hanging from the Heights of the Meirw side and with its thread swung back to its cave where landing it transformed itself into a Black Knight, who immediately raised his hand in salute to his former colleagues and laughing looked across to Corwen who was totally bemused by the spectacle she had witnessed. Wet and bedraggled the skeletal bones that had fallen made their way up the face of their cliff from the lake returning to their charnel house, whilst Curnan and the man behind him clambered up the hanging rope bridge to the trees on the Heights of the Meirw. There they were greeted by an excited dog and a beaming young boy relieved to see Curnan safely back. Curnan stretched out his hand to assist the man behind him, the last of the troop to cross. This soldier stood on the Heights of the Meirw and turning to Corwen signalled a farewell before removing his cap and muffler he revealed his golden hair and royal features. Curnan immediately knelt before King Arthur, who for a moment assumed the stature of a giant in his glory, with all the men who had arrived in the wood crying out his name, "Arthur, Arthur, Arthur," which echoed back and forth through the ravine. The King, before resuming the stature of a man once more turned towards Corwen and raised his hand. She signalled back and called on the waterfall to flow again before reforming herself into the white rock.

The shepherd boy, overawed, watched as the King took Curnan into his arms saying, "Come my Gawain, for it is you who has awakened me and who must now throw off the false name with which you have lived and be one with us in the work we must undertake." Curnan paid homage to the King and showing him the letter from Myrddin said, "Merlin only today revealed to me in this letter, that I am Gawain your Knight, having been released from Corwen's care many years ago so that I should be the one to ring the great bell and call you from your sleep at this time of need. Corwen vowed that I would have to prove my worth when this day came, by crossing the ravine with you and all your company in order to be with you on your quest."

They both looked back across the abyss once more before Arthur said, "Gawain, we all have work to do. But who is this boy standing here, and what has he to do with us?" Gawain explained all that the boy had done and who he was at which the King thanked the boy giving him a ring.

The boy promised to record the story for generations to come and left the Heights of the Meirw with the King and his Knights who were guided on their way by Gafallt. The shepherd boy returned to his home with Gafallt where he told his parents all that had happened showing them the King's ring which they told him to keep safe. He placed it on a long chain around his neck so that it would always be with him and yet, under his shirt, away from people's gaze.

One day soon afterwards, Gafallt became restless and ran towards the forest. The boy eagerly followed him since he knew that the dog had sensed something. On the out-skirts they were met by the elderly gentleman who had once instructed the boy to go to the inn to meet with Curnan. The man asked if the dog had a message for him. The boy took the note from Gafallt's collar and gave it to him who reading it asked, "So are they abroad in the world?" "Yes," replied the boy. "And did you meet the King?" "Yes, Sir, he gave me this ring." "All will be well, eventually," the man said, "but hide the ring in a place further back from Curnan's tree."

With that they parted company as Gafallt led the boy to the place in the forest where a root, marked with the letter "M" protrudes from a cliff and counting eleven trees back, the boy buried the ring, until it might be needed. Returning from the wood Gafallt stood still and the boy realised that they were to part. Sadly he gave a final hug to the dog which turned to the path that the elderly man had taken and ran off into the distance.

Three years later war was declared in Europe and the horrific suffering, the falling masonry, the fire and the blinding light that Curnan Reilly had seen in his vision on the liner became a reality. But the forces of good prevailed, peace was established and King Arthur and his warriors returned to Ogof y Meirw where they were joined by Merlin. As far as I am aware, the ring is still buried where the boy left it and as for the boy's name? It was Tag.

SOME WELSH WORDS

Welsh is a language of the British Isles with a literature and rich oral tradition which predates that of the English Language.

Arthur: There may have been an historical Arthur who was a Chieftain living in Britain in the early 6th century. His name may be a Welsh compound word, the first part of which "arth" meaning "bear"; the second part "gur/gwr" meaning man. As such it has been suggested that "Arthur" or "Bearman" could have been a rallying war cry. Others, however, suggest the name is of Latin origin from "Arcturus" which is the brightest star in the constellation next to the Great Bear, or from "Artōrius" a Latin name given to leading Britons.

Byw: alive, living.

Cadair: chair or throne.

Cadair Idris: the throne of Idris, a mythical Welsh god. Once a volcano it is a ridge mountain overlooking the Mawddach Estuary, with ten, or as some would claim, eleven peaks.

Caer:
castle or fort.

Corwen:
A compound word "cor"(sanctuary) + "maen" (stone). A linguistic mutation changes the "m" to "f". In the past "f" and "w" were interchanged, the "ae" became "e" so the word developed Corfaen, Corwaen, Corwen which translates as stone sanctuary or stone marking a consecrated spot. Today it is the name of a town in North Wales.

Cwm:
valley.

Cymru:
Wales.

Dafydd:
David, a popular Welsh name, the patron saint of Wales is Saint David.

Gafallt:
In an early Welsh tale, the name of the King's favourite dog was Cafall which may have come from the Latin word "caballus" meaning horse. Later the name was written as Gafallt.

Gawr:
a linguistic mutation is present here gawr: cawr, giant.

Mai:
May.

Marchwyn:
march: another word for a horse + (g) wyn: white.

Mawddach:
the name of a river and estuary in North West Wales known for its great beauty.

Meirw: the dead.

Morgen: some legends hold that Morgen was a spirit from the sea which in this story is transcribed to the wind coming from the sea bringing about tempest and storm. She is, however, a newly created character with a number of literary antecedents.

Morwen: môr: sea + gwen: white. Many Welsh names contain the element gwyn(masculine)/gwen(feminine). Literally it means white but has also an implied meaning such as beautiful, pure, blessed, shining.

Myrddin: Merlin.

Ogof: cave.

Penmaenpool: a hamlet below Cadair Idris in the Mawddach Valley. Penmaen literally means a prominent outcrop of stone/rocks and the pool (llyn) is a wide section of the River Mawddach. The full Welsh name is Llyn Penmaen.

Rhita Gawr: Rhita the Giant.

Seren: star.

Tanwen: tân: fire + (g)wen: white, whitefire.

Teifi: River in South Wales.

Tywi: River in South Wales.

Y: the.

REFERENCES

The Once and Future King

Malory writes, "Yet som men say in many p(art)ys of Inglonde that kynge Arthure ys nat dede ... and men say that he shall come agayne ... Yet I woll nat say that hit shall be'so, but rather I wolde sey: here is thys worlde he chaunged his lyff. And many men say that there ys wrytten uppon the tumbe thys: HIC IACET ARTHURUS, REX QUONDAM REXOUE FUTURUS" (Here lies Arthur, king once, and king to be). p.717, Marlory, *Works,* edited Eugène Vinaver, Oxford University Press, London, 1971.

Bear and Eagle

"Arthur ... /arth llu llewenyd dremynt/yr eryr ath welas gynt."

(Arthur ... /bear of the host, joy of sight,/the eagle has seen you before.)

Ymddiddan Arthur a'r Eryr, The Dialogue of Arthur and the Eagle, dating possibly from the twelfth century, see stanza 4, p.105, Jon B.Coe and Simon Young, *The Celtic Sources for the Arthurian Legend,* Llanerch Publishers, Felinfach, 1995.

MICHAEL KERR SCOTT

The World's Wonder

"Anoeth bid bet y Arthur," (The world's wonder a grave for
Arthur) *Englynion y Beddau, (Stanzas of the Graves)* date
of composition uncertain but included in the *Black Book
of Carmarthen,* (12th century) pp.100–1, Coe and Young.

The word "Anoeth" can be translated as a "marvel", "something difficult to find", a "wonder" or a "mystery".
This allows the phrase to have a plethora of differing
interpretations.

Dreams and Visions

"…there's a Lady Guinevere bears up that Sir Lancelot.
Dreams, dreams, visions, fantasies, chimeras, imaginations, tricks, conceits!" See I.iii, 53–5, John Marston, *The
Malcontent,* 1604, ed. M.L.Wine, Edward Arnold (publishers) Ltd., London, 1965.

Memory

"Cofio? 'Rwy'n cofio gormod. Ni does boen/Fel poen y
methu anghofio yn hunllef byw." (Remember? I remember too much. There is no pain/Like the pain of failing
to forget in the nightmare of being.) See Act IV, p.90,
Saunders Lewis, *Blodeuwedd,* Gwasg Gee, Dinbych, 1974.
Private translation by Eirlys Scott.

Printed in Great Britain
by Amazon

17772510R00109